D0463655

Dear Reader,

In 1982, my book *HOW TO SATISFY A WOMAN EVERY TIME* ... *and have her beg for more!* came out in hardcover and swept the country. I travelled all over during 1982 and 1993 doing TV and radio interviews, and the book sold 204,000 copies hardcover and was ten weeks on the *New York Times* bestseller list.

When I stopped promoting it, an amazing thing happened. It continued selling by word of mouth, around 10,000 copies a year.

Cut to 1990. *HOW TO SATISFY A WOMAN* was still selling by word of mouth without promotion and I thought to myself "It's doing nicely without me—I wonder if I can bring it out again and re-promote it so that more married couples can find sexual happiness and save their marriages?"

So I did in late 1991, and it really took off. By early 1992 it hit the *New York Times* bestseller list again and was on it for sixty-two weeks the second time around 1992 to 1993, (the only time in the history of the *New York Times* that the same identical hardcover book—not ever in paperback—came back years later on its bestseller list), and to date has sold over 2,000,000 copies in the U.S. In nineteen countries worldwide, it has sold over 600,000 copies and hit the bestseller lists in Australia and Germany, the two countries in which I promoted it.

Lots of people insisted I write *HOW TO SATISFY A MAN EVERY TIME* ... *and have him beg for more!* but

I thought that would be silly. Satisfying a man, I used to say, was so easy it was a joke. "All a man has to do is stand nude on his back porch and a little breeze could waft by and give him an orgasm."

But I was kidding on the square. I truly believed that men needed no help. It was almost impossible for a *woman* to have an orgasm through intercourse alone, and that's why *HOW TO SATISFY A WOMAN* was so incredibly successful, but men were blessed with a sex organ that aroused easily and climaxed easily.

Finally in 1996, the light bulb went on in my head. "If sex is so great for men, why are so many men cheating on their mates? If sex is so exciting for men, why are so many men getting divorces?" Then the ideas started pouring forth. The *psychology* of sex dominated me for weeks as the ideas started formulating.

And I have come up with many original ideas, a sexual technique, and a "master plan" for any woman who wants to *guarantee* that the man she loves will stay faithful to her because he will *never* be bored with her sexually.

It really works!

Koura Hayden

April, 1999

HOW TO SATISFY
A <u>MAN</u>
EVERY TIME . . .
and have him beg for more!

by
NAURA HAYDEN

KENSINGTON BOOKS
http://www.kensingtonbooks.com

PUBLISHER'S NOTE

Readers are advised to consult with their healthcare providers knowledgeable in alternative/complementary/preventive medicine to determine which vitamins, minerals and food supplements would be beneficial for their particular health needs and the dosages which would be best for them.

KENSINGTON BOOKS are published by

Kensington Publishing Corp.
850 Third Avenue
New York, NY 10022

Library of Congress Card Catalog Number: 98-067866
ISBN 1-57566-399-6

First Printing: April, 1999
10 9 8 7 6 5 4 3 2 1

Printed in the United States of America

To Love, which is Good . . .
which is Love . . .
which is Good . . .
which is Love . . .
which is Good . . .
which is Love . . .
which is Good . . .

God, with infinite wisdom, gave us the enchantment
of sex so that together we may joyfully pleasure each
other and create a loving bond that will last a lifetime.

Contents

Author's Note

You cannot have the quadruple whammy of physical, mental, emotional, and spiritual ecstasy unless sex is between two people who love each other.

I believe that sex and love belong together in a loving, faithful, committed, married relationship.

This is a marriage manual.

Foreword

Women do not understand why men cheat. There is enormous ignorance about men and sex.

Men don't cheat because someone else is better-looking. Men don't cheat because someone else is younger. A man cheats because sex becomes dull with his wife when she stops paying attention to his penis. She focuses on her kids, her house, her job, her friends, herself, but *not* on his penis.

We've all heard often enough that men don't understand women, but I think it's much more universal that women don't have a clue about the enormous importance of sexual excitement to men. I didn't say love and I didn't say sex. I said sexual excitement.

It's difficult for us to comprehend *how* important sexual excitement is to a male. His penis is an extension of his ego. It is the center of his universe, and his mental, emotional, spiritual, and physical selves revolve around this appendage.

Not to say he's totally aware of how important his sex organ is to him. I said *totally* aware, but he is definitely aware that his penis is king and reigns supreme over his life. Penis power to a man is much more important to him than we have ever been led to believe. And undoubtedly more important than he has ever thought, because he's probably never analyzed it before.

Of course your man knows you love him because you married him, and even though you may not often tell him or show that you love him, if you pay attention to his sexual needs, he will *feel* loved.

And when he feels loved and sexually satisfied, the reason for his fooling around outside his marriage has evaporated. Would you need to take an amphetamine when your body is bursting with health and energy? Would you need to take a sleeping pill at the end of a day in which you ran a 26 mile marathon?

Wives of men who have been caught cheating have always been considered the victims of their husbands' infidelity. Mrs. Nelson Rockefeller, Mrs. Albert Einstein, Mrs. Frank Gifford, Mrs. Norman Mailer, Mrs. David O. Selznick, Mrs. Artie Shaw, Mrs. John F. Kennedy, Mrs. Jim Bakker, Mrs. Robin Williams, Mrs. Bill Clinton, Mrs. Frank Sinatra, Mrs. William Paley, Mrs. Franklin D. Roosevelt, Mrs. Desi Arnaz, Mrs. Ted Kennedy, Mrs. Henry Ford II, Mrs. Charlie Chaplin, Mrs.

Mick Jagger, and about 200 trillion (if not more) wives throughout history have all felt sorry for themselves as we also felt sorry for them for having such unfaithful husbands.

An affair is nothing as simple as just a new body. If it were, a one-night stand would be all he'd need every once in a while. Every man wants to "fall in love", and that's why men risk everything to have an affair which is not a one-shot deal, but a sometimes long-term sexual relationship outside marriage that keeps the man excited.

It has to do with the depression of boring sex. It may appear shallow that the lack of exciting sex can cause overwhelming depression in a man's life, but his need for sexual excitement is so deep and so important to his mental, emotional, and physical well-being, that without it, life doesn't seem worth living.

What we women don't comprehend is how deeply depressed a man gets if his sex life has gotten boring. We hear about some man cheating and we think "Oh sure, he found some young thing and just because she's (younger, prettier, bustier, slimmer, etc.) than his wife, he had to bed her."

But that's not the answer. Sex with his wife had become so boring that he thought he'd go mad (or do away with himself) if he didn't find some sexual excitement.

So he did.

I am now convinced that it is the wife who is responsible for the husband's cheating. If she hadn't become complacent and allowed the sex to become boring at home, he wouldn't have been forced to look for exciting sex outside his home.

The lack of sexual excitement in a marriage is why there are so many divorces, and this is why I've written this book . . .

Introduction

I've been a big fan of Anthony Quinn's for years. He's always been a great film actor, but more than that, he was a man who knew how to have, and always appeared to be having, a great time. He was married in his twenties to Catherine DeMille, the daughter of the great film pioneer, Cecil B. DeMille, and had several children. Then he met Italian-born Iolanda on the movie set of *Barabbas* in 1961 where she was working as a wardrobe assistant, and they had two sons out of wedlock. Five years later when she was pregnant with their third son, they were married. Meanwhile, while married to Iolanda, he had a few other children out of wedlock. And of course several years ago, he had yet another child (he has thirteen kids to date!), this one with his former secretary, Kathy Benvin, and when the child was born and his wife found out about it, she went crazy, and demanded Tony leave her (he since had a second child with Kathy). He came up with what he thought was a great solution—Iolanda live in one part of their huge apartment on the Upper West Side of New York, and Kathy in the other part. Iolanda was understandably outraged, said no, and eventually filed for a divorce. She was heartbroken her marriage was over.

What's so obvious to most of us is that if Tony hadn't had the affair with Kathy, he would have had one with someone else and could just as possibly had a child (he obviously loves kids). It's not the girl's fault. Iolanda mistakenly thought he loved her so much that they'd be together forever. He undoubtedly *does* love her a great deal, but I believe his new wife must be making sex exciting for him, and that's why they're together.

And the same thing with Pavarotti. His wife Adua is very upset because Luciano's been travelling all over the world with his assistant, Nicoletta Mantovani, a young woman in her twenties. I believe it's not just because she's young, it's because she's making sex exciting for him.

Adua knows he loves her, the mother of his children, and he knows she's his best friend. But what she doesn't realize is how boring sex can often become to husbands after many years. Numbingly boring.

Most women believe that love conquers all. This is what most churches and philosophies teach, and love *is* the most important emotion of all. But what most churches and philosophies leave out is that romantic marital love is an active state, not a passive one, and must be expressed through its *deepest* expression, *sexual* love.

It's the same as if you really love music and you actively pursue great CDs and play them on a wonderful CD player with super speakers so the music will be heard to its best advantage. You don't passively listen to it on your decrepit tape player or dinky car radio. If you really love food, you actively pursue great restaurants and fresh, ripe fruits and veggies. You don't passively wait till someone maybe tells you about a terrific café or a new recipe. And if you love to read, you actively pursue great books and a very good reading light next to your bed. You don't only read books that happen upon you passively as you browse through a library or a bookstore.

So many of us love our husbands passively, but love of spouse is an *active* experience, and to be a *great* experience it needs the same dedication as love of music, love of food, love of reading, and any of the other loves.

Now love has many expressions. You can hug, you can kiss, you can hold hands, but again, the *deepest* expression of love is sex. Sex is a driving force, a life force screaming to be expressed—and if women understood this sex drive in themselves (forget for the moment their husbands), we would have fewer frustrated, angry, and tense wives. We wouldn't have so many terrible mothers who make their children's lives a hell on earth. My own mother was almost always

angry and took it out on me. Almost always, because
the rest of the time she was loving, but I was so afraid
of her terrible temper that I tensed up and stayed that
way for much of my life. She told me once before she
died that she had never had any pleasure in sex. She
said she had never had an orgasm.

No matter who a woman really loves, she will do
anything to make that person happy and keep that person
well.

We all know a woman's sacrifices for her children:
she'll get up early to make their breakfast, she'll pack
their lunches, she'll drive them to school, she'll take
them to the doctor and dentist, she'll go without to make
sure her children are well-dressed, healthy, and happy.

Now we all know not *every* woman is like that, but
most are. Some people are not really capable of deep
love. Maybe they were mistreated when very young and
this pain built up a wall to keep out any more pain, but
sadly the wall can't distinguish between good and bad,
so it keeps out *all* feeling. That's what fear brings with
it.

Certainly there are neurotic, sick and disturbed
women, but the majority of us are ready, willing and
able to give and receive love.

We don't usually take our kids for granted—we know
they need us at all times, they need our help and love
on a constant basis. But oftentimes we do take our
husbands for granted. Sex becomes functional—we do

it because we know we have to in our marriage. But many of us, if we really had a choice, would give up sex altogether. This is because we, the wives, do not always, if ever, have the great pleasure of an orgasm. Many of us make love (actually we allow our husbands to make love), and because of our passivity, we don't make it exciting. We lie there and let him "do his thing," thinking that's all we need to do to keep him sexually satisfied. But alas, he is soon super-bored sexually with his unimaginative, bored wife (anything would get boring if one of the partners is bored), and it's pretty obvious wifey, who's doing it by rote, is more than bored—she honestly would do almost anything *not* to have to make love with him.

"Not tonight honey, I have a headache, stomachache, my period, I'm tired, etc., etc., etc." Obviously, if she knew the top of her head would come off in an incredible orgasm of intense pleasure in less than ten minutes without any struggle, frustration, great effort and enormous expenditure of energy on her part, her headaches, stomachaches, period, tiredness, etc., would disappear in a flash. In fact, they would never have been there in the first place 'cause she would have been thinking about her exciting body-pleasure-to-come during the day and she would be thrilled to have her husband initiate sex. And if he didn't, she would.

Ah, but that's my *other* marriage manual.

We were all meant to have sexual pleasure with our

bodies. That's why a woman's sex organ (clit) is there for pleasure. A man must orgasm to procreate, but a woman can have twenty children *literally* and never have an orgasm. The clitoris is a part of her body that is there *only* to give her pleasure, only to deepen the love she already feels for her husband, because hopefully he's the one giving her the orgasm.

If a woman loves her husband for many other reasons (he's smart, he's funny, he's loving, he's affectionate, he's thoughtful), she will forget herself for the moment and concentrate on keeping *his* sex life exciting. Because when she's got him panting for her (even after five, ten, twenty, forty and more years), she will be in a position of great strength, and he will do almost anything she wants (learn to make incredible love to her). And that's the beginning of a *truly* great marriage when two people who really like, love, and respect each other have great sex every time they make love.

If a woman *really* cares about her husband and/or *really* wants their marriage to last, she'd be wise to revise her thinking and try to understand that, if the love is still there, sex is the *cement* that keeps that marriage glued together. Not just sex, but *exciting* physical, mental, and emotional sex, and when a woman gives that to her husband on a daily basis, no amount of TNT or no H-bomb could blow that marriage apart.

And a wife's age has nothing to do with it. Most

people tend to think that all a woman has to be is younger to wrest a man away from his wife. Not true. It may seem so because every day many more young women enter the work force out of high school and college, so youth abounds, and many men wind up with younger women.

Look at Prince Charles who left his thirtyish wife, Princess Diana, for his fiftyish paramour, Camilla Parker-Bowles. And his uncle, the Duke of Windsor, 42, who became King Edward, forsook a gorgeous, much younger woman in her early twenties, Gloria Vanderbilt's aunt, Lady Thelma Furness, to marry Wallis Simpson, who was forty, and for anyone who's ever seen her photo, not a beauty. In fact, she was rather homely, but with mucho money and good taste; she dressed exceedingly well and became at least stylishly attractive. But she obviously had strong sexual power over King Edward for him to have given up his throne for her when they married in 1936 (and he and she then became the Duke and Duchess of Windsor), and their marriage lasted their lifetime.

What attracts a man is a woman who thinks he's sensational, and if his wife has started taking him for granted and a younger woman at work treats him like a king, anything could happen and often does.

All a man really needs to know and feel is that his wife truly loves him *above all* and will do anything and everything to make him happy. A wife can be *any* age and if she cares enough and has learned how, she can sexually captivate her man.

I don't care if two people are married for two years or forty years, it is absolutely possible for a woman to enchant her husband so much sexually that he'll *never* feel the need for another woman. Obviously, a wife has to really love her guy and be willing to learn what to do to keep him enchanted, but unequivocally I state it can be done. Read on . . .

1
Why Men So Easily and So Often Get Bored Sexually

Every man desires and needs sexual excitement every day of his life.

It doesn't have to be actual physical sex every day (although that is the ultimate ''high'' for a male), it can be just the thought of someone who turns him on that brings the excitement.

Some men sublimate their sexual energies into socially constructive or creative channels. Others deflect their biological urges into business transactions. But the basic sexual needs and desires are there.

What seems like just a small part of his anatomy and his life actually controls his mental and emotional well-being.

I am going to liken a man's need for sexual excitement to a diabetic's need for insulin. If you give a diabetic a daily dose of insulin, the diabetes is controlled and he is healthy. If you give a man a daily dose of oral sex, his need for sexual excitement is controlled and the marriage is healthy.

If you *don't* give the insulin, the man will die of diabetic coma. And if you don't pay attention and focus on the man's penis, the marriage will die of marital coma.

Having an orgasm is the greatest physical pleasure on this planet—bar none. And it's very simple and easy for a healthy man to orgasm, so it's no wonder he'd like it as often as he can get it. But if he's married and his wife has lost interest in sex, boredom will set in.

I don't mean boredom with sex, I mean boredom with the person he's sexing *with*.

When a man's mate is too sure of him and fails to keep sex exciting, he will look around for excitement. It's as simple as that.

Many wives know their husbands love them and know they're their husbands' best friends. After living together for many years, having kids, sharing the joys and the pains, the love is very strong. But what so many women don't realize is how boring sex becomes to males if you just expect him to put it in, pump away, and quickly orgasm. That would be infinitely worse than eating only dry toast at every meal in a very small room with no windows. Now when you're starving, the toast would be a treat, but otherwise—BOR-RING!

In a recent Women's Health Conference in Washington, D.C., research showed that men have sex to feel physical pleasure (surprise!), and most women have sex to strengthen the relationship through sexual intimacy.

All men want sex. Most want it often. And that's because it *is* such incredible pleasure and the pleasure comes so easily to them. And it also makes them feel so good and so "UP" afterwards (lots of endorphins kicking in!).

If women had as easy a time orgasming as men do (feeling the incredible pleasure), we would seek sex as relentlessly as they do. But we don't because it's very difficult—almost impossible without my technique—for a woman to orgasm during straight man-on-top intercourse, and the other ways (oral sex, hands) are not *nearly* as exciting and fulfilling as the "missionary."

The difference is that a female orgasm with oral sex or hands is only around the genital area, the sex organs, whereas a female orgasm with intercourse makes every nerve ending in your body explode—your knees, your elbows, your legs, your arms, your neck, your shoulders, your stomach—*every* nerve ending!

So because sex doesn't come as easy for us, we many times relegate it way down on our priority list. Almost everything becomes more important than sex: kids, new furniture, clothes, hair style, having a good figure, manicure, new car, terrific diet, great movie, exciting job, fabulous apartment, and the list goes on with sex near the bottom.

Now men all want more or less the same things as women do, but their priorities are different. Sex would be at the *top* of the list, not the bottom.

And when women *really* realize this, we will actively become great lovers. I'm talking both *technically and psychologically* great lovers.

To drive a man wild, insane, crazy in bed (assuming that you love each other in the first place) will guarantee that relationship will last. When the sex is constantly exciting, he will think about you when you're not there and want a replay as quickly as possible.

Many feminists will scream that no woman should *ever* have sex with a man just to please him, that that's demeaning to womanhood. They say it has to be always *mutual* pleasure. But when a wife really loves her husband, look at the great pleasure she would feel giving her beloved much needed love (an oral sex orgasm) every day or as often as possible. Goodness *is* its own reward!

And look at other aspects of life, particularly work. If you can't wait to leave the office and are out the door at 4:59:59, or if your focus is not on your work and you take lots of personal calls on company time, do you think your boss will treasure you as a valued employee? A working woman with a boss might stay late in her office to finish a job because she knows that will make points with her boss and help get her promoted. And if a woman is running her own business she might take a client out to dinner, even though she really doesn't want to, but she knows that when she does go out of her way for the client, the client will be more likely to be loyal to her business.

How is this different from pleasing or not pleasing your husband? If you know promptness is important to him, is it loving for you to meet him thirty minutes late? And if you know he desires and needs a lot of sex, why not cater to his pleasure? If you do it in your job and you do it for your kids, why not do it for the man you love and married?

Feminists tend to have a problem whenever sex comes into the picture. When my book, *HOW TO SAT-ISFY A WOMAN EVERY TIME . . . and have her beg for more!* came out, feminists picketed a bookstore in San Francisco. They were outraged with my title (which I loved because the ''begging'' is amusing to me, but most feminists are not known for their great senses of humor!)

The *really* amusing part is that the *Los Angeles Times* printed a question from a reader asking if any lesbians were buying the book. And when I saw the reply, that yes, some bookstores had reported that, I started asking booksellers if that was their experience. Many said yes, that even though the huge preponderance of buyers were heteros, there were some lez couples asking for it, which only goes to prove that no matter what your sexual proclivity, everyone who cares for someone is looking to learn how to satisfy that sexual partner.

I definitely consider myself a feminist—I've always supported myself, I believe in equality in every area, I bought my own house, etc. I've never believed that men are better than women or that women are better than men. Some women are smarter and some men are smarter—it's an individual thing. But most men are sexually needier than most women, and women must understand this to coexist happily in a male/female world. I also believe in the power of sex in marriage. Everybody knows the power of *love* in a marriage, but not everyone understands how powerful sex (the deepest *expression* of love) is.

I've read of two situations with two different couples that I found very enlightening. The first was a story in *Vanity Fair* (a *great* magazine) "The Screenwriter: Not Your Average Joe" about one of the most successful screenwriters in Hollywood, Joe Eszterhas, who was married to Geri and had a teenage son and daughter with her. He has written many big screen hits including *Basic Instinct,* starring Michael Douglas and Sharon Stone. In the spring of 1993, he and his wife had a houseguest for several weeks, Naomi Baka Macdonald, whose husband had left her for Sharon Stone, and she was recuperating emotionally at their house. Naomi says that Geri had gotten "lost in her children . . . she didn't see a lot of things that she should have seen and could have seen.'' When the three of them would go someplace in a car, Naomi says that Geri would encourage her to sit in the front seat of the car with Joe. ''He likes talking to you,'' Naomi says his wife would say. Geri, the wife, even encouraged her to buy a short black silk robe, saying, ''Joseph would love it on you.''

Is it possible anyone could be or would be so naive and so blind to reality? In a short period of time in the midst of Naomi's stay, Joe left Geri, moved in with Naomi, divorced Geri, married Naomi, and then had two children with her. Joe says, ''that his ex-wife feels that Naomi is a demon.'' As I see it, she's not a demon, and Joe would not have fallen in love with Naomi if their marriage had been satisfying.

The second situation I read about in a wonderful book, *Haywire*, by Brooke Hayward, daughter of a very famous show-biz couple of the 1940s and 1950s. Her father, Leland Hayward, was one of the biggest actor's agents of his era (he discovered Henry Fonda and Jimmy Stewart, and represented many of the top Hollywood stars like Greta Garbo, Judy Garland, Gregory Peck, Fred Astaire, etc.) and then later became a producer of some of the greatest Broadway shows (*Mr. Roberts, Gypsy, Sound of Music,* etc.), and her mother, Leland's wife, Margaret Sullavan, was a star on Broadway (*Stage Door, Voice of the Turtle, Sabrina Fair,* etc.), and a Hollywood star (*Little Shop around the Corner* with

Jimmy Stewart, *Back Street* with Charles Boyer, etc.). They had three children and were very happy together.

His work was mainly on the West Coast in the film biz, and she hated Hollywood, so she took her own money and bought a house in Connecticut and lived there most of the time with the kids, her husband flying back whenever he could.

She was so upset when she found out that he was fooling around in her absence (what did she *think* he would do when she deliberately left him alone for weeks on end?), that she decided to test their marriage and do a play in London for six months, even though her husband *begged* her not to go, and told her how vulnerable and lonely he was at that time. Quoting Leland from the book, "Basically, I'm absolutely monogamous. Basically romantic. Faithful. As long, that is, as I know I'm cared about."

While his wife went to England, he took another woman, Slim Hawks, ex-wife of director Howard Hawks, to Hawaii (which news devastated his wife—again, what did she *think* he would do for six months alone?), and when his wife came back from England, they got a divorce. Everyone who knew them at that time all agreed that Maggie had an arrogance of wanting things the way *she* wanted them without thinking of or caring about what her husband needed or wanted. He eventually married Slim Hawks, who later *also* left him alone for long stretches of time, and they eventually divorced. He then met Pamela Churchill, who *really* knew how to love and keep a man (see next paragraph). If both his wives left Leland alone so much, you can imagine how important they must have thought sexual pleasure for their husband was. This kind of arrogance and complacency is the bottom line to why so many couples split.

Any and all women really successful in love relationships know and practice giving their lovers great and loving sex. The recently deceased Pamela Digby Churchill Hayward Harriman, one of the twentieth century's great paramours (if not the greatest), who married three extraordinarily successful men, had long-term and intense relationships with some of the most powerful men in the world: Randolph Churchill (Winston's son) whom she married, William Paley, Jock Whitney, Edward R. Murrow, John F. Kennedy, Aly Khan, Gianni Agnelli, Elie Rothschild, Leland Hayward, whom she married, and Averill Harriman, whom she also married. Obviously, she knew the overwhelming power of sex. She also was very caring and nurturing of whatever man she was with, so with great love and even greater sex she conquered some of the most powerful men of this century.

Whenever there's no fun, no surprise, things get boring. Think of any movie that bored you—you knew what was going to happen next and you couldn't wait to walk out of the theater, and you probably did before it was over. Think of people you know who bore you. They repeat and repeat the same things over and over, you never hear an original thought from them, and when you spot any of these dullards walking toward you, you know they're going to corner you and you'll be trapped and have to listen to tedious, uninteresting, obtuse, tiresome conversation. So you either pretend you see someone you know across the room, wave and walk away. Or you talk for several minutes and then say you're going to get another drink, hors d'oeuvres, coffee, or anything you can *think* of to get away.

Well, that same boredom is what happens when a man realizes that sex with his spouse has gotten to the point of putting it in, pumping a few times, and coming into a wife who's even more bored than he is, but at least she just has to lie there.

He, as a male, has to first desire his wife's body, get excited, and then ''do it.'' Now sometimes he's so horny he could do it to a knothole, but I'm not talking that. I'm talking about his normal, everyday life when he needs mental stimulation to ''get it up.'' And if that stimulation ain't there, he's going to go looking for it, because sex is very important to him.

And he might not even have to go looking. There are lots of women out there who can sense when a man is looking, and you really can't blame her for being there when he needs her. It is *he* who gives out (consciously or unconsciously) the initial signal, and she responds.

Believe me, when a man is happy sexually at home and truly satisfied by his one and only (and not at home alone or on the road alone travelling for weeks at a time), *no* woman can seduce him.

You're going to find out what you can do to absolutely *guarantee* to keep him un-bored and sexually stimulated, satisfied, and faithful to you . . .

2
What Every Man Is Looking For

You can't seduce a sexually satisfied married man—you can't break up a sexually exciting marriage.

Everybody is looking for the same thing—to fall in love and to stay in love. Not to say that men are aware of this. Men are usually only aware of sex, sexual attractions, and sexual feelings; most just don't know that falling in love always starts as a sexual attraction, and the sexual pull must be there or he can't and won't fall in love. And only if the sex (or the promise of it) is exciting for him will he keep the relationship going which thereby gives love a chance to happen.

Now when a man falls in love, that *guarantees* sexual excitement for him. As long as he's in love, he'll stay sexually excited and as long as he's sexually excited, he'll stay in love.

If a wife would realize that any woman (from a mistress to an affair-ee to a co-worker) who cares for a man and who's sexy and pleases that man, works at it. Any woman who seduces a wife's husband (who signalled that he could be had), focuses on what will make him really happy sexually and then she does it.

Why doesn't a woman who loves her husband do the same focusing? "My wife doesn't understand me" is not a cliché or a joke. She really *doesn't* understand her husband's sexual needs.

It's so foolish to just assume (because you feel his love) that your husband loves you so much that you know he'll never leave you. What complacency! What arrogance! Of course he loves you, but if you allow yourself to become so complacent that you get too sure of him, you might be surprised (shocked?) to find he's secretly been looking for some excitement.

The one absolutely, positively infallible way to keep his life with you exciting is sexually. If you've made sex so exciting to him that he can't wait to have you "do" him again, he's not going to be giving off signals to any hot tamales in his workplace that he's not sexually tied to someone at home.

Women *always* blame the "other woman," but again, you can't seduce a sexually satisfied married man. If you are a great cook and make a good breakfast for him every morning, whip up great delicious dinners every night, make sure his clothes are always washed, cleaned, and pressed, keep the house looking neat and clean, keep yourself spiffy-looking at all times, take really good care of the kids, and let him always know you love him with hugs and kisses, but let him get bored with you sexually, you're in for some trouble.

Of course he loves you, he loves you a lot, but he'll be vulnerable to any and all hot-looking babes who may or may not make the first move. If he's open for excitement, *he* probably will give off the first signals and you can't blame her for responding to his cues.

If he does fool around and you find out about it, it will probably be a shock to you and you'll feel sick about it. You may even be so upset you'll ask for a divorce. Unfaithfulness is many times the end of the trust in a relationship and leads to the end of the marriage.

And of course the sex may be *so* great with the woman he's cheating with that he's willing to give up everything he loves to keep the sexual excitement she brings to him going on every day of his life.

I knew a man many years ago who travelled a lot to Chicago on business, and one night he brought a woman he'd just met back to his hotel room. In the middle of the night the phone rang and the woman, in her sleepy haze, answered it. It was the man's wife calling from New York, and the wife was so shocked that she hung up. He got the hotel operator who said it was a woman asking for him, so he knew for sure it was his wife, and he knew for sure that his wife, a very smart cookie, knew he was cheating.

He called her back and tried to tell her she got the wrong room, but she told him their marriage was over and not to come back. She said she would pack all his belongings and ship them wherever he wanted, but she never wanted to see him again. He was so upset he asked the woman to leave, he called the airline to find out the first plane the next morning back to New York, he packed, checked out and went directly to the Chicago airport. From the airport at dawn, he called several business associates and left messages saying he had an emergency and had to cancel that day's appointments and would call them from New York later that day.

When he got home, she had the chains on all the doors and wouldn't let him in. He begged her, but no soap. He told me he got semi-hysterical and was physically sick with remorse for having done this to his wife and to himself. She told him she wanted a divorce and never wanted to see him again.

He finally moved into a hotel later that day and bombarded her with phone calls (this was before everybody had answering machines). He said he was so distraught he couldn't eat or do business.

After several weeks (and he lost twenty-three pounds) she agreed to have dinner out with him to discuss the divorce. Because he felt he couldn't live without her, he convinced her of his great love and asked her to forgive him. He swore it would never happen again because he would never go anywhere without her. He said that he looked so haggard and sick that she took pity on him and said she wanted to think about it.

Finally she took him back and he kept his word and never travelled again without her. I didn't see him for many years, and then one night at a restaurant in Los Angeles I saw him. He introduced me to his wife, a rather unattractive woman (looks don't have an awful lot to do with a strong sexual hold), and they looked very happy together. The next day he called and filled me in on what had happened since I last saw him. They decided to change their lives totally, so they moved to Los Angeles right after they went back together and then sold their house. He said she started to pay a lot more attention to him sexually than she ever did before, and that their marriage got much stronger *because* of his one fling.

A woman friend of mine, married for over thirty years (and happily she thought), was looking for her husband at a party. Told he stepped outside for some air, she went looking for him and found him in a parked car necking with a girlfriend of hers. She was shattered, but because they were both Catholics, she forgave him and tried to forget it. She tearfully asked me *why* would he do that when they love each other so much and for so long? I considered not telling her the truth, but after some thought, I decided I had to.

"Because sex with you had become so boring," I told her. When I asked her when was the last time sex was exciting for *her,* she couldn't even remember. She told me she never had an orgasm with what she called "regular sex," but she proudly said she never faked it. I asked her what she did and she said she just laid there.

"Boy, that must be exciting for *him,*" I said. She'd never thought about her boredom boring the bejeesus out of her husband. She thought that just "putting it in" was exciting enough for him.

I told her there's gotta be *fun* in sex, the same kind of fun you have when you play an exciting game like charades or tennis or poker. You never get bored when you're having fun, so when you make *sex* fun, your partner will never be bored, and neither will you, and when he's really turned on by you, after you've given him the greatest orgasm he's ever had, you'd be amazed what he'll do to make sex incredible for *you!*

Why are games fun? Because everything is a surprise. With charades, you have no idea what the person is going to act out; with tennis, you don't have a clue where your opponent is going to hit the ball; and with poker (or any card game including solitaire), you don't know what card is coming up next. Surprises are not only fun, they're exciting.

So to make sex exciting, I told her she'd have to surprise her husband and take charge of his body—

really take charge of it—and think of things that would drive him wild and crazy and insane in bed (Chapter 9 coming up!).

She later told me he was shocked when she announced she was taking charge, that he became totally passive and let her do *whatever* she wanted. The part that shocked *her* was that in all the years of their marriage he had always been in charge of *everything* in their marriage and seemed to love it, but when she took over sexually, he went *crazy!* In fact, he wanted her to do it often, that's how much he liked it.

She said he began to relax more with not having to be The Big Boss all the time. And sex was *definitely* not boring anymore. She had so much fun with his passivity and her taking charge of his body and exciting him to the point of climax and then stopping (which *really* is a sign of POWER!) until *she* decided it was the right time to give him his orgasm.

Again, a man does not fall in love with and leave his wife for another woman because she is younger or prettier than his wife. It's because she is more *exciting* than his wife. It just happens that she's sometimes prettier and sometimes younger, because usually younger people are more receptive to new ideas, more willing to try new things, and that makes them more exciting. Married women often are lulled into a false sense of security. ''I know he loves me and the kids and he'll never leave us.'' But the truth is she's stopped focusing on her husband. All she talks about is the kids or local gossip or things only interesting to her, and he's bored out of his skull. And if wifey thought about it, she would be bored too if hubby talked about things only interesting to him. The reason *she's* not bored with him (and hey, she *may* be bored) is that he's living an exciting life, thinking new and exciting thoughts, and meeting lots of new and exciting people. And one of those exciting people is HER. Her age is irrelevant to him. She could be older than he, she could be his age, or she could be younger. But she is *always* exciting to him. Their conversation is exciting, she's on the same level as he, whereas wifey sometimes thinks and acts (and feels!) like he's the star of the family and she's just a supporting player.

When I was down in Australia in 1992 with *HOW TO SATISFY A WOMAN <u>EVERY</u> <u>TIME</u> . . . and have her beg for more!,* I read an excerpt in a magazine of a book by Noelene Hogan who was married to Paul Hogan and was now his ex-wife. If you saw the film *Crocodile Dundee* you know how charismatic Paul is, and he had fallen in love with an actress, Linda Kozlowski, divorced Noelene and married Linda, who happened to be younger and more beautiful than his wife. But after reading part of Noelene's book in the magazine, I can understand why he left. Noelene is very sweet, unassuming, pretty, but with zero self-esteem.

Paul had a habit of not introducing me to people.
I would stand there like a lily on a dirt bin and
feel totally insignificant. I remember the first time
I met Stuart Wagstoff. He and Paul were chatting
away and yours truly was standing there not having
been introduced. I could see Stuart was slightly
uncomfortable but I was new to all this show biz,
so I just stood quietly by. Finally Stuart said: ''Are
you Mrs. Hogan?'' I looked at the floor and mum-
bled I was. When I looked up again Paul and Stuart
had moved off.

Now it might appear that Paul was mean to her, but
you must remember that *people accept you at your own
evaluation.* If a wife sees herself as a timid little nothing
who has no value but the love she feels for her husband,
her husband isn't going to value her either. Throughout
their marriage, he was the king and she was the serf
100 percent of the time. That cannot *ever* work! The
excerpt was full of put-downs like her husband sarcasti-
cally telling her how pretty she looked as she scrubbed
the floors in old clothes and her hair in curlers. At a
certain point she says ''Gone is the timid little house-
wife,'' but alas, it's too late.

Several years ago I went looking for a houseboat.
Ever since I was a kid and was crazy about Huey, Dewey
and Louie, Donald Duck's three nephews, I dreamed
of living on a houseboat. *They* were on a houseboat and

the fun never stopped, so I thought "when I get grown up, some day *I'll* have a houseboat too!" Over the years I looked and I even went to boat shows. I went to one in Australia and there wasn't even one houseboat. Hundreds of yachts and sailboats, but not one of what I was looking for.

Then I found out why. After finding a boat dealer in the Yellow Pages and going out to Long Island in New York to see a houseboat, the dealer said that the reason no one wants a houseboat anymore is that you can't go anyplace on it. There's no motor on it, it's a barge with a box sitting on it which you live in. He showed me a forty-foot motor yacht that was like a houseboat except there were different levels (a houseboat cabin is flat) and you could travel on it on water to almost anywhere you wanted.

I then changed my mind and decided a motor yacht would be terrific, but I'd have to wait 'cause they're a lot more expensive. The dealer told me he'd like me to see just one more moored at the marina, so I took a look. Wow! It was fabulous. Fifty feet with everything a person could ever want on a boat. Unfortunately I didn't have enough money, but it's definitely in the future.

The fellow who owned the fifty-footer was very warm and personable and through our several-hours visit, he told me about himself. He used to be married and has two grown sons. When he and his wife divorced a few years ago, he'd bought this boat (he'd loved boats since he was a kid) and lived on it ever since. He said he had a girlfriend and he said she was in her thirties (he was in his fifties). I asked about his ex-wife, and he said he's crazy about her and goes down to Key West on his boat to see her several times a year. I said it looks like you still love her and he said yes, he loves her as a friend, and they have so much in common too, but he doesn't want to be married to her because the woman he now dates is very sexy.

I asked him if he had a lot in common with her too, and he said no, hardly anything, but the sex was great. He said she didn't like boats or water (which he obviously adored) and even more importantly, she didn't like animals. He had a Persian cat, Michelangelo, who was not only adorable but brilliant—he taught himself to turn a door knob with his two paws and get into any of the cabins. The owner showed me by closing the stateroom door and in about twenty seconds Mikey opened it and walked in. Mikey knew that this man's girlfriend didn't like cats, and one night he peed right in one of her expensive shoes. Very smart cat!

Now I asked him how could he be with a woman who hates cats, boats, and water, the three things he loves the most, and he said, "Her lovin' makes up for everything." And it does, unfortunately (or fortunately, depending on your viewpoint). Millions of people get married because of sexual attraction, and when that wears off, as it almost always does because most people *let* it wear off, they find they have nothing in common, and go looking for another sexual attraction.

You wouldn't take a lifetime job you're not suited for just because you love the looks of the office, but it's very similar to marrying someone who turns you on but with whom you have nothing else in common.

What you *should* do is wait till you find someone who has the same values, same sense of humor, same likes and dislikes, marry that person and make sure that both of you learn how to satisfy a man/woman every time and have him/her beg for more!

Those are the marriages that will last a happy lifetime!

To make a living, people work their tails off. They get up early, rush to make sure they're not late, spend eight hours a day focusing on their duties, sometimes stay late to finish a job, put up with job-related jealousies, back-biting, catering to the boss—all to make a buck.

Now you have your marriage, which is a love-job. But few of us ever treat it with the same respect we treat a job. In marriage, we usually expect (and want) the other person to do most of the work. If we could just see how silly and foolish that is (and we can if we compare marriage to work), we might be able to focus the same energies on our relationships as we do on our jobs.

At the office do we *not* expect each person to clean

up the kitchen/dining area after he/she uses it? I've seen enough signs around demanding that slobs clean up or don't come back! But how many of us leave the kitchen/ bathroom/bedroom in a mess and expect spouse-o to be the servant? Don't we make an effort at the office to be pleasant even when we don't feel terrific? But at home we feel free to snarl, be rude, be selfish—things we wouldn't and couldn't get away with at the office. Probably the third time you snarled at the boss, you'd be fired, and you know that, so you make an effort to be nice. That same effort will go a long way at home.

I believe the reason so many married people don't value each other more is because sex becomes less than great after a few months and years of marriage. When the sexual excitement goes, so does the need for sex with that person go. The respect comes back when the need returns, and that happens when your beloved asserts his/her power over you with sex so exciting that you again can't live without it.

A woman absolutely can keep her husband faithful, keep him from cattin' around, and keep him wanting sex with her and *only* her throughout his life.

Would you ever think of cheating on your guy, the man you love and are married to, if he knew exactly which buttons to push to turn you on sexually? If he were in charge of your body and you never had to say "a little to the right, honey," "not so hard, sweetheart," and he was able to *make* you have an orgasm whenever he wanted to, would you *ever* think of another man?

As you read my book you will begin to understand that part of my "faithfulness credo" is a *physical* technique, a way to work your husband's body and pleasure it so intensely that he'll want it as often as you'll give it to him.

Another part of my "faithfulness credo" is a psychological technique, a way of literally captivating (capturing?) him so intensely in the mental and emotional realm that he will *literally* be your captive.

And once you capture him you will let him know that for you to continue being his captor, he has to learn how to capture *you* (that's my *other* marriage manual!). Nothing in life or marriage can be one-sided. If things aren't fair, they don't work.

Now you probably noticed in the above that I used the word "work," but even though some work is difficult, other kinds of work are not only easy, they're so much fun that you wouldn't even think of them as "work."

When you give great pleasure to someone, the feedback is so immediate and intense that you will receive mental and emotional pleasure. When you're in charge of a project (decorating your home, planning a party, capturing your husband sexually), the feeling of power that you're not only doing the job, you're succeeding fabulously in it (your home is gorgeous, the party was a smash, and your husband is totally dependent on you for sexual excitement and satisfaction) is the headiest kind of self-confidence that exists.

Now obviously if you're married to someone whom you no longer love or who no longer loves you (and it's irretrievably over because drug addiction, violence, serious character flaws, a new awareness of having no basic compatibility, a realization that she doesn't *really* love you anymore, etc., are present), then you should get out as soon as you can.

This book is for wives who truly love their husbands, love making love to them, and want to keep them faithful forever . . .

3
Why Some Men Get into Kinky Sex

If you're not in love, sex can still be a feel-great physical experience. An orgasm but not much *real* excitement beyond physical pleasure. An orgasm is sexual surrender, and how do you totally surrender to a stranger, or a wife who's no longer loving, or someone you don't think is terrific enough to fall in love with?

Now some men are afraid of love, afraid to surrender to a woman—*any* woman—and these are the men who frequent prostitutes. Just pay the money, take off your clothes and let her "do" you.

A man can be married and have five kids and still be afraid of the surrender that being in love demands. When a man's not in love, he needs much more stimulus to have an orgasm. A guy can be *in like* with his wife, love her dearly, but not be *in love,* with the accompanying great sexual attraction that goes with romance.

So he cheats on her and gets the temporary excitement

of a new face and a new body and maybe his stimulus is his imagination with this new body, and that does it. Maybe he wants to be spanked or maybe he wants to do the spanking.

When love is missing, lots of "incidentals" are needed to make the sex exciting. Sometimes pain is needed as a stimulus. And it can start out solely imaginative pain, as with a velvet whip. You can only imagine the humiliation of having the velvet hit your flesh, because there won't be any pain.

But as time goes on, the velvet whip loses its excitement. Real pain is needed to stimulate the sexual response. A man will seek out real whips and a woman who's into S&M, and the pain must gradually increase to keep sex exciting.

Without love, there is a constant need for more pain and dirtier magazines and tighter chains.

A few years ago when I started dating one of the biggest radio stars of all time (and he was hoping we'd be a romance), he told me his turn-on. As soon as I heard it, I was turned off, but we did remain friends.

To look at him you'd think *macho*—tall, dark wavy hair, very handsome—but he was into submission to a female dominatrix. His fantasy was crawling on his hands and knees toward his woman/master and grovelling at her feet. And that's *all* he wanted to do, he did not want to reverse roles or do anything else *but* grovel.

This guy, so charming and so successful but so unable to give real love, could only be excited by a woman putting him down. He had been married and had a daughter, and he truly broke his wife's heart. She loved him so much but he, for whatever reason, was unable to deeply love her back. He craved humiliation and was only happy when he got it. He never told his wife about his sexual needs, maybe because he didn't think she could dominate him because she loved him so much, or maybe he was afraid or embarrassed to tell her, but it's a shame, because every woman *could* play out this scene, and maybe if she had known and made it like a game, just maybe he could have again been sexually excited by her and stayed with her, and maybe she who loved him dearly could have gotten him to try some *other* sexual games.

Another man, one of the biggest political tycoons of all times was also the head of an American political dynasty. He was one of the wealthiest and most powerful men in this country, and he was also a sexual sadist. But he had enough money to cover up his sadism, to pay a show girl at the Latin Quarter in New York in the late 1930s an enormous sum so that she allowed him to beat her up frequently. He also paid her rent for a suite in a New York midtown hotel for several years, and during each visit he inflicted so much injury on her that he had to have a nurse stay with her in the room for several days after he physically abused her.

This particular woman was a friend of a close friend of mine and she told him how this sadistic man would punch her and beat her up, and one day my friend was in the hotel and saw this man emerge from the elevator and walk through the lobby with a hat on, overcoat collar up, and a false nose (a false nose!!!). Just from my reading knowledge of him with his large and famous family, and particularly with his long-suffering religious wife, it was pretty apparent that he was incapable of real love.

He also had a long-time affair with a famous actress and she told stories of his cruelty and dishonest financial dealings. My favorite story was when he dumped her after years of being together, and then stole some of the money back from her that he had previously given her. Whattaguy!

Can a person be loving and cruel? Can you be tender, gentle, and sadistic? A person can *act* the loving virtues and be a tyrant, but *real* love displaces any and all cruelty.

One of the giants of the Big Band Era, who had a great band and dozens of hit records, was married and divorced several times. He had some strange sexual aberrations, one of which was giving dinner parties at his home, and as the guests ate at the large and long dining table, he had a girl under the table *doing him* while everyone ate. When she was finished she'd crawl out and of course everyone was shocked (he laughed and loved it), and he got a reputation with those who knew him well as a *very kinky cat.*

Many times those men who are extraordinarily rich or famous or both have sex thrown at them by "groupies" who are eager to go to bed with them. When a man does not have incredible sex at home, and has dozens of women throwing themselves at him (particularly when he's travelling), it's so easy to have sex with a different woman every night (and many times more than one!). And lots of these groupies will do wild and crazy things, and a man, not caring a whit for any of these women, could easily get into kinky stuff.

Some men get their kicks with a *ménage à trois*—two women and a man interacting. Or some men want to just watch two women make love, or watch another man and woman make love. Or participate in an orgy where everyone is sucking and intercoursing with everyone else. Besides the obvious disease possibility (probability?), the men needing this are constricted emotionally. They are not able to give or receive real love. They are only seeking physical pleasure, and with love out of the picture, a lot of mental stimulation is needed to get it up. Pain, humiliation, animals, and punishment are just some of the mental "naughty things you're not supposed to do" that are temporarily exciting. Why would a man need two or more women when he only has one penis? I know there are other things he and they could do, but the bottom line is the orgasm happens with his penis, and the rest of it (the two or more women, etc.) is only to make sure he gets excited enough so his penis *will* orgasm (which would happen automatically and with the *ultimate* pleasure if he were in love).

But what if he's depressed because of a repressed childhood with his mother and father, or his church's teachings, or someone who got to him with some negative impact, frightening him emotionally? If he's not able to open up totally to one woman and feel that quadruple whammy of physical, mental, emotional, and spiritual soul-mating that this kind of total ecstasy brings, he would be wise to seek counseling to get to the root of his inability to love and be loved.

Sex without love is not fulfilling. It may be temporarily exciting and make the body feel better by getting rid of tension and releasing endorphins, but the mind and soul and spirit are empty. Kinky sex never grows in and of itself; it always needs more and stronger stimulation, whereas sex with love (naturally where both spouses have orgasms) always grows more exciting just *because* of the love.

As men get older and dissipate through drinking, smoking, eating too many rich and junky foods, having too little exercise, or all the above, the wonderful sex diminishes because their bodies diminish. So physically they may need more and more stimulation. *Playboy* centerfolds, *Penthouse* pictorials, *Screw,* porno flicks, etc.

It's a sad but true fact that as most of us mature and grow older, our bodies change and sometimes not for the better. Most get weaker as we age, but some of us who work at it get better as we get older. If we never took care of our bodies in our youth, if we never exercised and we ate lots of junky foods, we went downhill. Then, as we start recognizing that our bodies are starting to fail us as we grow older, we start to exercise and really make an effort to keep out sugar, booze, cigs, caffeine, etc., we *can* get stronger, our skin *can* get ''juicier,'' and we *can* look and feel much younger.

But for those who do not treat their bodies as temples of God, their sex drives start to slow down. And it takes more and more stimulation to be aroused and to orgasm. There are many reasons for this. One is a person's circulation. Of course it's an individual thing, but if your blood isn't flowing as easily as it once did because now you have excess cholesterol and plaque taking up a lot of room in your veins and arteries, or your heart isn't pumping as strongly as it once did, your penis will not engorge with blood and get as rigid as it used to.

And even though the desire may be there, if the body doesn't respond to sexual commands, a person might logically feel that more mental stimulation is needed. So all kinds of fantasies run through your mind, and maybe some very kinky thoughts are included in the hope that maybe the wilder the kinks are, the faster the erection will happen. But when your body is not in great shape, Marilyn Monroe could come back in person nude at her most gorgeous time of life, and nothing will happen to your penis. But if your body is healthy, just *thinking* about a nude female body will arouse you, and your penis will respond to your sexual desires without any outside prodding necessary (see Chapter 7 re: ginkgo biloba, vitamin E, and CoQ10 which will all help your heart and circulation—and no matter what your age, it's *never* too late to start!).

The bottom line is that when your body is really healthy, *that's* when sex is the most pleasureful and the erections are the most rigid and satisfying to your woman (and to you!). And if you stay healthy as you get older, sex without kinks can become more and more satisfying for both you and your woman.

But the very most important thing to know is that when you truly fall in love, kinky sex is replaced by an overwhelming desire to kiss and hold and make love in a normal fashion with your beloved. Because making love in a normal fashion with your beloved is the most exciting sex there can and will ever be.

4

The True Sense of Being In Love

Loving and being "in love" are two completely different states.

Loving can be compassionate or caring, or both.

Being "in love" can be compassionate and caring, but it *must* also be sexually exciting, which loving does *not* have to be.

You can love your sister, brother, mom and dad, and your kids, but you can't be "in love" with any of them unless you have an incestuous relationship.

When you are in love, your beloved is your sexual master, the "one who has the power of controlling" you (Webster's dictionary). Being in love is a touch of masochism for both parties. To truly be in love is to feel like a love slave—powerless in the hands of your beloved.

But this power over you is something you consciously and willingly give to your beloved. She does not make you her slave—*you* make yourself her slave. Willingly and happily.

Because someone is your sexual master doesn't mean that the person is necessarily aware of this. Remember *you* have made her your master through your imagination and your innate desire to *have* a sexual master.

Because you feel you don't want to live without your sexual master you get married. At first married life is great and your sexual master turns you on. Sex is great at the beginning because in your mind she *is* your sexual master and definitely in charge of your body. She is a goddess and you are in awe of her hold on you. She has incredible sexual powers that she uses with you, and you love the feeling of being under her power. It makes you super-sexy.

Because she's not aware that she's your sexual master, she thinks the power she senses she has over you is just the strong love she feels from you—and the fact that you want to make love often. She knows you need her body.

But she's wrong. You don't need her body. There are millions of female bodies in the world, dozens in your world, and you're not interested in only a body.

You want someone to take charge of your body—not your life, not your mind, not your money—but your body. You want a sexual master. *That's* the turn-on. And because she's not aware of this, she can't understand why, after a while, you're not as sexy around her as you once were. She senses you're getting bored, but she doesn't know why. And neither do you.

All you know is you start telling her you're tired, you've been working hard all day, and you honestly don't *want* to make love as much as you used to.

Once a man has made the decision that your body and soul are the only body and soul that he wants to merge his body and soul with, he is in love.

And once you let him down and don't keep his body and soul excited with the promise of great body-and-soul-exploding sex on a constant basis, he will make the decision (consciously or unconsciously) to fall out of love with you.

He will probably still love you if you still love him, but he won't be "in love" with you anymore.

Maybe he will still love your soul, your mothering abilities, your personality, your sweetness, and maybe even your brain.

He will still need your help in making him feel comfortable, cleaning up after him, your presence in his life. That is, he will need you until he finds another woman who excites him sexually. When that happens, he won't need you anymore. He will still love you if you're not too angry and if you allow him to still love you.

But he won't still be *in love* with you.

Think of people you know who are really in love. Now think of famous people you've read about who have stayed in love with the same person all their lives. What do they have in common? What's different about them?

- Bess and Harry Truman
- Georgiana and Ricardo Montalban
- Clark Gable and Carole Lombard
- Alma and Colin Powell
- Betsy and Walter Cronkite
- Helen Gurley Brown and David Brown
- Lydia and Charlton Heston
- Renée Taylor and Joe Bologna
- Veronique and Gregory Peck
- Nancy and Ronald Reagan
- Gloria and Jimmy Stewart
- Ellin and Irving Berlin

All these couples are (or were) together and in love for their lifetimes.

Why have they stayed in love? What do (or did) they as couples all have in common? First, each partner clearly looked up to and respected the other.

Harry, a very strong person, always called Bess *The Boss* when talking about her, and for the President of the United States to put his wife on that kind of pedestal shows the kind of respect he had for her.

Clark and Carole weren't married a long time when she died in a plane crash during World War II, but I've always felt they would have lasted through thick and thin. She called him "The King" and he always said she made him feel like one.

I don't know about the intimate details of the sex lives of these people, but I'd bet a bundle they enjoy or enjoyed sex a lot with each other. You just *know* that Renée and Joe are lusty bed partners. And I have my own private visions of Harry (a rather small man) just losing himself *literally* with his beloved Bess (a very big woman) when they went to bed.

I'd bet another bundle that Helen and David have now and have always had an active and exciting sex life 'cause Helen is super-aware of the importance of sex in all of our lives, and she's written about it in the books she's penned.

There's no doubt in my mind that she sexually satisfies her husband, bringing her own unique focus that she uses in everything she does from exercising every day to watching her diet to having helmed *Cosmopolitan* (aka *Cosmo*) to sex in her marriage.

These couples all have or had wonderfully happy and successful marriages which lasted all their lives. And not one of the couples ever had any gossip about infidelity on either part. They obviously loved each other, but do you think two people could live together thirty, forty, fifty years without sex being a strong part of that marriage? I don't. You'd get on each other's nerves and there'd be so much tension and friction that the union could never last. And that's where sex comes in—relieves tension and creates a *pleasure bond* that can and will carry two people through all kinds of problems and keep the sparks of love alive.

Why else were we created with this incredible sex drive? Certainly sexual pleasure is the impetus for a male to reproduce, but again, a woman can literally have fifteen children and never have an orgasm. So that great sexual pleasure a man is capable of giving his wife was *only* given her for pleasure, and is a pleasure-bond that assures that she will only think of sex with the man who gives her that incredible sexual pleasure every time they make love.

One of my all-time favorite jokes I just saw in a story about cheating, "The Perils of Adultery" by A.J. Benza in *Playboy.* I've always liked the joke so much that I put it in my movie *P.K.,* a wacko, zany comedy that I hope to release soon. Unless it escapes first. *Ba-da-bum . . .*

Eighty percent of all married men cheat on their wives in this country. The other twenty percent cheat in Europe. *Ba-da-bum . . .*

I'll tell you why. Because we're men, plain and simple . . . Can I be frank? It's a dick thing. And sometimes there's no explanation other than what a famous comedian once told me: You show me the most beautiful girl in the world, and I'll show you a guy who's tired of fucking her.

This is the whole point of my book. If a woman is passive as she's made love to, boredom soon sets in. No matter what she looks like, how old she is, how much a man loves her. Passivity is boring. Once a woman learns to be *actively* involved, she can hold her guy in thrall for as long as that marriage lasts. But if she remains sexually passive, her guy will eventually cheat.

Most men are not aware of why they are cheating, and those who are aware are afraid to tell their wives the truth about their cheating. They pass the responsibility to the women they had the affair with. "She seduced me," "She really made a big play for me," etc. By doing this, their wives never find out that they're cheating because sex is so boring at home. And anything boring certainly can be changed.

No man can be seduced unless he wants to be. And the truth is that the man always gives out signals (staring at a woman's breasts, touching her arm as he's talking, saying that sex is not big-time for him anymore, etc.), or actually making the first move.

I have had dozens of married men make a play for me, and I *never* came on to them first. Each one, in his own way, let me know he wanted to have an affair. I used to get very distressed to see how many married men were obviously unhappy and wanted to fool around.

At that time I didn't understand how utterly important sexual excitement was to a man, and I desperately wanted to see happily married men who didn't fool around. I wanted to know that it was possible, but there were very few. The only time I ever did come on to a married man was many years ago, and I didn't know he was married. I asked him to my house and he declined, telling me he was married. I was so happy I found a married man who was faithful, but I was ignorant then because I thought men cheated just to be cheating. I thought it all just started with them wanting to fool around. I didn't look for the cause and effect. Now that I'm smarter and wiser, I realize his wife was one smart cookie who made *sure* he was sexually satisfied at home. There was no *reason* for him to fool around.

Donald Trump said that Marla told him he'd have to work at keeping their marriage going, and he said that he has to work all day in his business and he doesn't want to have to work in his marriage. Now for my big question: why didn't *Marla* work at the marriage by continuing to do what makes Donald happy and changing herself rather than trying to get *him* to change?

Somebody has to start the work of making the marriage better, and if the woman starts to make the sex more exciting, she might be amazed at what her husband might do to make the marriage grow better.

My *HOW TO SATISFY A WOMAN EVERY TIME . . . and have her beg for more!* came out in Holland in late 1996 and I went there for TV, radio, magazine and newspaper interviews, one interviewer, Jan Heemskerk, from an important national Dutch magazine, *Man,* started asking me questions about *men* and sex. When I told him I was just writing *HOW TO SATISFY A MAN EVERY TIME . . . and have him beg for more!* our discussion got very animated. Every statement he threw at me I had covered. He said many women feel that if they love a man, that's all it takes to keep him faithful, and I of course brought up Tony Quinn and Pavarotti. Then he said that many women feel that their husbands try to barter with them for sex, and these women again feel that their love should be enough to keep their husbands happy and faithful. It was a very exciting discussion for me because he verified all the things that I instinctively felt were misunderstood by the majority of women.

Then he said that my *HOW TO SATISFY A MAN EVERY TIME . . . and have him beg for more!* was going to be *more* important than my *HOW TO SATISFY A WOMAN EVERY TIME . . . and have her beg for more!,* and here we disagreed. He said (and correctly) that because a man orgasms so easily, women think that's all that's important to him. I agreed that just having an orgasm doesn't necessarily make exciting sex, but I pointed out that even though having an orgasm isn't always exciting, it's better than *never* having an orgasm. And there are millions of women who have never had an orgasm, or have hardly ever had one. So because of this difference, showing men how to make their wives orgasm every time is urgently important to keeping a marriage happy. So I believe the two books are equally important.

Certainly showing women how to keep sex exciting to their husbands is *just* as important to a happy marriage, and that's why I've written this book.

One of the most important parts of sex between two people who love each other is to have fun, to make it a game.

You notice how games keep kids from getting bored? If you're going on a long car trip, you start planning some games to keep them occupied mentally before they start complaining and kvetching about "How much longer," "Why is it so long," "When will we get there," etc.

Mothers do all kinds of things to keep their kids from getting bored but they think their adult husbands are beyond having to keep interested. Wrong! The minute your relationship starts getting boring, that's the minute he starts looking around. And when your relationship is getting boring, you can bet that sex with you is not thrilling to him.

Naura's credo:

> Love is never a game!
> Sex is always a game!

The bottom line to mutually exciting sex is to become each other's sexual slave and each other's sexual master, and to have *fun* with it.

At one sexual interlude the wife may be the sexual slave and the husband is the sexual master. And then the next time the husband is the sexual slave and the wife is the sexual master.

When the wife is the sexual slave she allows her husband to be the sexual master and take control of her body. He is totally in charge and will tease her body until she is half mad with desire and then, when he feels he wants to, will make her have an orgasm. (See *HOW TO SATISFY A WOMAN.*)

When the husband is the sexual slave he allows his wife to be the sexual master and take control of his body. She will be totally in charge and will tease his body until his penis is throbbing, and then when she decides (and *only* when she decides) it's the right time and she wants to do it, she will make him have an orgasm. (See Chapter 9.)

This is the biggest turn-on to every man and every woman—to lose control over your sexual body—to have the person you love and trust totally control you sexually.

And when you have a sexual master, you will never think of sex with someone else. Your sexual master has made you a sexual slave—and when your sexual master makes you have an orgasm, that is the *ultimate* pleasure, the same feeling as when you first fell in love and that beloved was your sexual master. You weren't *aware* your beloved was your master, but she was. And he was.

So now you're *aware* of becoming a sexual slave, and that will make your sexual pleasure exciting as long as your beloved continues being your sexual master. And of course you must also continue being a sexual master when the roles are reversed.

It's a game. And it doesn't have to take a lot of time if you don't want it to. If a wife wants to make sucking her husband's penis a game, she can drive him wild with desire by teasing his cock with her tongue for several minutes, and then making him orgasm sooner rather than later.

The whole event could take five minutes. But it brings real pleasure every single time you make love. And isn't this what each one of us is looking for? And we've been looking for this our whole lives.

But what if your mate is not the playful type, thinks sexual master and sexual slave is silly and refuses to play the game? Maybe there's a lot of repression there and not only in sex. It could be from a number of reasons possibly going back to childhood. Maybe he's physically not in good health and he could have anxiety or even depression.

If he doesn't have any of these problems, he's just not into fun and games, you'll have to play the game by yourself. All it takes is a little *extra* imagination. You can be his master sexually without his even knowing it—you just take charge of his body and if he rebels (the fool!), you stop your lovemaking. Eventually (very soon) he'll get the idea. And eventually he will play the game because he'll find out that if he doesn't, he won't get any. And don't let him bring you down by negatives ("Stop," "This is ridiculous," "I don't want to") because when you've *really* taken charge, everything he says will roll off your back *because* you're the sexual master (if only in your own mind).

He will find it exciting because it's reality—he'll begin to realize he *made* you his sexual master when he originally fell in love with you. He wasn't aware of it, of course, but that's the reality, and all you're doing is becoming to him what you were originally, the woman he adored, treated with kid gloves, and wanted to spend his life with. There are some control-freaks who don't think of their mates as their sexual masters, and of course their spouses are *only* sexual slaves, but these relationships are sick to begin with and won't (can't) last.

The "soul mate" he's *really* looking for is his sexual master.

5

Sex Survey of Married Men

Before I wrote *HOW TO SATISFY A WOMAN EVERY TIME ... and have her beg for more!*, I did a sex survey of married women. I was only interested in married women because I believe that the true pleasure of sex belongs in a committed, loving, faithful relationship, and that is almost always in a marriage.

This first survey had 486 women participate and the results surprised me. That's when I found out that in intercourse all women fake it some of the time and most women fake it all of the time.

Before the survey I had faked it all through my marriage and I honestly thought there was something wrong with me. I thought maybe I was frigid, maybe it was a physical problem, or then again maybe it was mental or emotional. I knew there was nothing wrong with my husband—*he* had an orgasm every time we made love.

Finding out there was nothing wrong with me made

me feel normal and terrific because I sure felt awful thinking I was abnormal and not-terrific all the years I was faking it. This was a few years before my *HOW TO SATISFY A WOMAN* book came out and I had not yet found out with my survey of married women that almost all women fake orgasm during intercourse, so I had no way of knowing I wasn't the only one doing this. Up till finding this out I thought I was the only one, so I was truly relieved to find there was nothing wrong with me, to find out that it's a universal female problem. The survey helped me a lot, and my book was the first one that let women know that they weren't alone in their faking it—all of us did.

From what I learned in that survey came the foolproof technique showing husbands how to *make* their wives have orgasms through intercourse *alone* (no hands, no oral sex, just intercourse done a little bit different) and from that I wrote my *HOW TO SATISFY A WOMAN EVERY TIME* . . . *and have her beg for more!*

The first survey was in 1981. Then ten years later I did a second survey of women, and this time I interviewed 1,102 married women and it was enlightening in a different way. I found out how much women want their mates to take charge of their female bodies and what a turn-on that is to both sexes.

And now that I finally wrote *HOW TO SATISFY A MAN EVERY TIME* . . . *and have him beg for more!*, I've done another survey, and it was sent to 510 married men. I'm printing the survey so you will see the questions, and I will give you the percentages of men who answered each question either yes, no, or more in depth.

The answers tell you what men *really* want sexually in their marriages . . .

SURVEY OF MARRIED MEN

This is a survey in which your identity is anonymous. You will not sign it, and no one will ever know that you filled it out.

Please be as frank and as completely honest as you can be. Your truthful answers will help millions of married men realize that they are not alone, that their problems are shared by millions of other married men.

Thank you for taking the time to participate in this very important marriage survey.

Naura Hayden

NAURA HAYDEN

Author of: *HOW TO SATISFY A WOMAN EVERY TIME* . . .
and have her beg for more!

Soon to be published: *HOW TO SATISFY A MAN EVERY TIME* . . .
and have him beg for more!

PERSONAL DATA:

I am White _____ Black _____ Hispanic _____ Asian _____
Other _____.

I now live in _____, _____.
                      City   State

SURVEY OF MARRIED MEN

1. How long have you been married? _____

2. How old are you? _____
   Month, Date, Year_____

3. Are you a religious person? _____ What religion? _____

4. How many times have you been married? _____

5. Have you ever been unfaithful in *this* marriage? _____

6. Have you ever thought about being unfaithful? _____

7. If you ever cheated on your wife did it affect your marriage? _____

8. Do you have children? _____ How many boys? _____ How many girls? _____

9. Does your wife ever use oral sex with you? _____ How often? _____ Did she offer to do this the first time, or did you ask her to? _____

10. Do you have an orgasm every time through oral sex? _____

11. Does your wife ever use her hands to bring you to orgasm? _____

12. Have you ever masturbated? _____ When you have, do you always have an orgasm? _____

13. Do you smoke? _____ How much? _____ Do you drink? _____ How much? _____

14. Do you masturbate since you've been married? _____ How often? _____

15. Has sex with your wife ever gotten boring to you? _____ If so, why? _____

16. In intercourse do you always have an orgasm? _____

17. What is your favorite way of lovemaking? Mark 1 as your favorite way, 2 as second favorite way, 3, etc.

    Intercourse (man on top) _____
    Intercourse (woman on top) _____
    Oral sex—giving _____
    Oral sex—receiving _____
    Other _____

18. Do you love your wife? _____ Are you in love with anyone else besides your wife now? _____

19. Do you *like* your wife? _____

20. Do you feel an emotional intimacy with your wife? _____

21. Do you use oral sex on your wife? _____

22. During intercourse, would you prefer to be on top or do you prefer your wife on top? _____

23. Do you feel that affection (hugs, kisses, etc.) is *as* important as having an orgasm? _____

24. Do you feel your wife is sexually selfish? _____ Are you? _____

25. How old were you when you first made love? _____

26. How old were you when you first had an orgasm? _____

27. Do you feel your wife is concerned that you are possibly not sexually satisfied? _____

28. Do you think your wife has ever faked an orgasm with you? _____
Do you think you'd be able to tell if she were? _____

29. Do you think that some women may be naturally "frigid"? _____

30. Have you ever wanted to make love but not been able to because you couldn't get an erection? _____

31. Have you ever lost an erection during love-making? _____
Do you have any idea why? Alcohol, drugs, fatigue? _____ Other? _____

32. Do you think you are a good lover? _____
    Why? _____

33. Are your best orgasms during intercourse (you on top)?
    _____ Intercourse (wife on top)? _____
    Fellatio? _____ Masturbation? _____
    Other? _____

34. Do you think your penis is a good size? _____

35. Do you sometimes orgasm too soon after penetration? _____

36. Have you ever gone to a prostitute? _____
    Did you enjoy it? _____

37. Does pornography turn you on? _____

38. Do you like anal stimulation, her fingers or tongue? _____

39. Do you like giving your wife oral sex? _____

40. Do you like stimulating your wife's clitoris with your hand? _____

41. Have you ever told or shown your wife what to do to you to make sex better for you? _____

42. Are you affectionate? Very _____ moderately _____ hardly _____ not at all _____

43. Is your wife affectionate? Very _____ moderately _____ hardly _____ not at all
    _____

44. Do you think a man can be happily married without having sex often? _____

45. How often would you like sex? _____

46. Would you like your wife to give you oral sex every day? _____

47. Do you think it's just as important for a woman to have an orgasm as it is for her husband? _____

48. Do you consider yourself happily married? _____

49. Do you think your wife is happily married? _____

50. Are you happier as a married man or were you happier single? _____

51. What about marriage do you like best? _____ _____

52. Would you like your wife to take sexual control of your body? _____

53. Would you like to take sexual control of your wife's body? _____

54. Would you like taking turns being in charge of each other's body? _____

55. Is your wife your best friend? _____ If not, who is? _____

56. If you didn't know your wife and you met her as you are today, would you marry her now? _____

57. Why did you get married? _____
_____

ANSWERS TO SURVEY OF MARRIED MEN

1. How long have you been married? ___from 8 mos.___
   to 57 yrs. (average) 9⅔ years

2. How old are you? from 17 to 86 (average) 34½ years
   Month, Date, Year _____X_____

3. Are you a religious person? _____67%_____
   What religion? _____X_____

4. How many times have you been married? 1 X 70%—
   2 X 26%—3 or more X 4%

5. Have you ever been unfaithful in *this* marriage?
   ___63%___

6. Have you ever thought about being unfaithful?
   ___97%___

7. If you ever cheated on your wife, did it affect your marriage?
   ___72%___

8. Do you have children? _____92%_____ How many
   boys? _____X_____ How many girls? _____X_____

9. Does your wife ever use oral sex with you? ___77%___
   How often? _____(average) 1 X every 5 wks_____
   Did she offer to do this the first time, or did you ask
   her to? _____12% offered 88% asked her_____

10. Do you have an orgasm every time through oral
    sex? ___37%___

11. Does your wife ever use her hands to bring you to orgasm? _____16%_____

12. Have you ever masturbated? _____100%_____
    When you have, do you always have an orgasm: _____98%_____

13. Do you smoke? _____42%_____ How much? 1 pk 97% _____ Do you drink? _____96%_____ How much? _____(average) moderately_____

14. Do you masturbate since you've been married? _____100%_____ How often? _____(average) once a week_____

15. Has sex with your wife ever gotten boring to you? _____82% yes_____ If so, why? _____X_____

16. In intercourse do you always have an orgasm? _____81% yes_____

17. What is your favorite way of lovemaking? Mark 1 as your favorite way, 2 as second favorite way, 3, etc.

    1—Intercourse (woman on top) _____67%_____
    2—Oral sex—receiving _____24%_____
    3—Intercourse (man on top) _____6%_____
    4—Oral sex—giving _____2%_____
    Other _doggie style 1%_

18. Do you love your wife? _____83% yes_____
    Are you in love with anyone else besides your wife now? _____X_____

19. Do you *like* your wife? _____82% yes_____

20. Do you feel an emotional intimacy with your wife?
    __84% yes__

21. Do you use oral sex on your wife? __92% yes__

22. During intercourse, would you prefer to be on top or
    do you prefer your wife on top? __wife on top 94%__

23. Do you feel that affection (hugs, kisses, etc.) is *as*
    important as having an orgasm? __56% yes__

24. Do you feel your wife is sexually selfish?
    __35%__ Are you? __30%__

25. How old were you when you first made love?
    __(average) 17__

26. How old were you when you first had an orgasm?
    __(average) 15__

27. Do you feel your wife is concerned that you are possibly
    not sexually satisfied? __52%__

28. Do you think your wife has ever faked an orgasm with
    you? __42% yes__
    Do you think you'd be able to tell if she were?
    __93% yes__

29. Do you think that some women may be naturally
    "frigid"? __87% yes__

30. Have you ever wanted to make love but not been able to
    because you couldn't get an erection? __59% yes__

31. Have you ever lost an erection during lovemaking?
    __72% yes__

    Do you have any idea why? Alcohol/drugs, fatigue?
    __48% 30%__ Other? __stress 22%__

32. Do you think you are a good lover? __92%__
    Why? __always wait till satisfy wife__

33. Are your best orgasms during intercourse (you on top)?
    __9%__ Intercourse (wife on top)? __47%__
    Fellatio? __39%__ Masturbation? __5%__
    Other? _____

34. Do you think your penis is a good size?
    __91% yes__

35. Do you sometimes orgasm too soon after penetration?
    __72% yes__

36. Have you ever gone to a prostitute? __14%__
    Did you enjoy it? __92%__

37. Does pornography turn you on? __85% yes__

38. Do you like anal stimulation, her fingers or tongue?
    __76% yes__

39. Do you like giving your wife oral sex?
    __94% yes__

40. Do you like stimulating your wife's clitoris with your
    hand? __100% yes__

41. Have you ever told or shown your wife what to do to
    you to make sex better for you? __87%__

42. Are you affectionate? Very _____ 61% _____
    moderately _____ 38% _____ hardly _____ 1% _____
    not at all _____

43. Is your wife affectionate? Very _____ 67% _____
    moderately _____ 32% _____ hardly _____ 1% _____
    not at all _____

44. Do you think a man can be happily married without
    having sex often? 13% yes

45. How often would you like sex? _____ every day 94% _____
    _____ 3 X week 5%   2 X week 1% _____

46. Would you like your wife to give you oral sex every
    day? _____ 100% yes _____

47. Do you think it's just as important for a woman to have
    an orgasm as it is for her husband? _____ 98% yes _____

48. Do you consider yourself happily married?
    _____ 79% yes _____

49. Do you think your wife is happily married?
    _____ 79% yes _____

50. Are you happier as a married man or were you happier
    single? married 92% yes

51. What about marriage do you like best?
    _____ companionship, sex often, kids _____

52. Would you like your wife to take sexual control of your
    body? _____ 100% yes _____

53. Would you like to take sexual control of your wife's body? _____100% yes_____

54. Would you like taking turns being in charge of each other's body? _____100% yes_____

55. Is your wife your best friend? _____68%_____ If not, who is? _____buddy, male friend 32%_____

56. If you didn't know your wife and you met her as you are today, would you marry her now? _____63% yes_____

57. Why did you get married? _____fell in love 98%_____

6
Some Very Important Male Health Info

Health is everyone's most precious possession, and all of us, both males and females, must do everything in our power to stay healthy and energetic (health and energy *do* go together!). Men have a particular part of their bodies which needs *special* attention and that is the prostate. I've researched and found some extraordinary natural plants and herbs which can help males keep an extra-healthy prostate without drugs.

But before I tell of these wonderful natural substances, let's get into male anatomy.

The external male sex organs are the penis and the testicles. The testicles are inside the sac called the scrotum. Penises and testicles come in many different sizes and shapes, and the only time I have ever been with a man whose penis was *unusable* was when I was very young and at that time rebellious after my religious schooling that said *no sex before marriage,* so naturally

I had to find out as often as I could what all the brouhaha was about (I have since agreed that love and commitment *are* the prerequisites for *incredible* sex).

This particular man had the largest penis I have ever seen. It was over a foot long and my fingers couldn't touch when I put my hands around it. He was the envy of every man who ever saw him in a men's room, but the truth of the matter was he couldn't have intercourse with anyone and no woman could ever get it in her mouth or anywhere else. He was extremely good-looking, tall with dark hair, and very successful as a "garmento" in the fashion industry in Los Angeles, but never married and hardly ever had sex, and that only when a woman stimulated him with her hands. He was truly a pathetic case.

So much for *that* old wives' tale!

Back to male anatomy: during an erection, the spongy tissues around the penis become engorged with blood making the penis bigger and more erect. There are no muscles in a penis so it can't be made bigger by any kind of exercise.

The head of the penis is the most sensitive to most men, particularly the part that connects the head to the shaft.

The internal sex organs are the testes which produce both sperm and testosterone, the male sex hormone. The vas deferens are the two tubes which extend from the testes to the prostate, and the sperm, having travelled through the tubes, is stored at the top of the tube until they mix with the secretions from the prostate and seminal vesicles just before ejaculation. The prostate secretes seminal fluid, and only a tiny percentage of this is sperm. The urethra is a tube from the bladder which goes through the penis and ends in a tiny hole at the bend of it. Both urine and seminal fluid go through the urethra, but never at the same time. The prostate wraps around the urethra right where it begins at the bladder, and that's why many men over fifty have urinary problems when the prostate enlarges, compressing the prostatic urethra causing the obstruction of urine flow from the bladder making urination difficult and sometimes painful.

Too many of my male friends have had prostate problems, and I want to quote one of the finest medical doctors in the United States, who is very much into preventive medicine, John A. McDougall, M.D. In an article in *Veggie Life,* he explains that routine prostate examinations have never been proven to reduce the risk of cancer.

> Understanding the growth rate of cancer will help explain why early prostate cancer detection and treatment are of limited value.
>
> Prostate cancer begins with one malignant cell. This transformed cell grows and divides into two cells at a steady rate—called the doubling time. For prostate cancer cells (as well as most other

solid tumors) the average doubling time is approximately 100 days. In other words, four malignant cells would be present in the prostate after 200 days, and only twelve cells would have formed after one year.

In six years, the cancer mass would contain one million cells (about the size of the tip of a pencil). A mass of this size is undetectable by PSA, digital rectal examination, or ultrasound. In essentially every case, by this time the cancer has already spread to other parts of the body. Only after an average of ten years does the mass grow to a size detectable by present day techniques. At this point the disease has most likely spread to the liver, lungs, bones, and brain, soon resulting in death. Therefore, routine screening does not improve the patient's outcome.

The American Cancer Society released guidelines advising individuals to avoid all red meat because of its very strong link to colon and prostate cancer. They also recommend following a diet high in fruits, vegetables, and whole grains. A low-fat, pure vegetarian diet is our best defense for preventing prostate cancer, and may actually slow its progress even after the cancer has started.

I've been a vegetarian for over twenty-five years, and I'm bursting with health and energy. Unfortunately some people think vegetarianism is weakening, and that we humans need to eat meat to be strong, but that's totally incorrect. The strongest animals in the world, elephants, are vegetarians, as are hippos and rhinos, and one of the fastest animals in the world, the thoroughbred race horse, is also a vegetarian.

I stopped eating all meat and fish because I love animals and abhor cruelty to and killing of all beings, but the side effect for me has been incredible good health. It was a bonus, because at that time I hadn't a clue that eating meat was bad for you. Who knew back then? But now we do know, and fortunately lots of people are giving up animal protein and biting into faux sesame chicken, soy hot dogs (with mustard on a bun), pseudo beef with orange sauce, sunshine burgers (with tomato, onions, and mustard on a sesame seed bun)! Talk about delicious! And what about barbecued marinated portobello mushrooms? They're one of my all-time favorite dishes.

So when you decide to give up eating animals for eating veggies, you'll discover a brand-new world of truly delicious foods. Plus you'll start getting healthier than you've ever been.

A healthy prostate is one of the most important parts of a strong male sexuality. It's also vital to good reproductive function.

But by the age of fifty, half of the male population will develop prostate problems. And over the age of sixty, seventy-five percent of men will have developed enlargement of the prostate gland, called benign prostatic hyperplasia, or BPH, which is caused by a buildup of testosterone in the prostate. This in turn is converted to dihydrotestosterone, DHT, which stimulates the cells of the prostate to multiply excessively. As the prostate grows larger it presses against the urethra, which starts to obstruct the urine flow from the bladder. An almost constant need to urinate (especially at night), burning sensation while urinating, weak urinary stream, dribbling, and feeling that you can't urinate "all the way" are symptoms of BPH.

However, there are lots of natural plants and herbs that can reduce these prostate disorders. Often hormone imbalances can create prostate problems and some non-toxic plants, saw palmetto for one, can produce hormone-like activity thereby correcting the imbalance. And the wonder of plants and herbs is that there are no side effects as there can be with many drugs.

Two of the biggest-selling prostate medications on the market have as some possible side effects: impotence, decreased libido, dizziness, and lightheadedness. And the FDA (Food and Drug Administration) recommends that one of them, because of its toxicity, never be used if a man will be ejaculating into a woman of childbearing age because of the possibility of a male fetus developing birth defects. Scary, no?

Saw palmetto is a small palm tree which produces

berries, and the reddish-brown powder is a natural treatment for enlarged prostate. Many men over forty start using it as a preventive and that's a very good idea. Saw palmetto extract is safe, and no negative effects have ever been reported in clinical trials. It relieves the BPH by preventing the conversion of testosterone to dihydrotestosterone, thereby not allowing the prostate cells to multiply and keeping the prostate from enlarging.

Saw palmetto is also getting a reputation for stimulating hair re-growth, so you not only help your prostate, you might also help your hair follicles.

Pumpkin seeds are another natural treatment for enlarged prostate, particularly when used with saw palmetto. A quarter to a half cup of raw pumpkin seeds, (a big handful) eaten every day along with one 500 mg capsule of saw palmetto with each meal can be very beneficial. Some men take two 500 mg capsules with each meal for a more intense dose.

Obviously a healthy life-style is important along with a good diet, little booze, no cigs, and lots of exercise (even ten to fifteen minutes a day is excellent). Vitamins and nutrients after meals is also important. In the next chapter, I list all the vites and mins and antioxidants that a body needs every day to stay well and healthy, and I also list how many I take, which is more than most people take, but not too many people have my energy and feel as good as I do (dare I say hardly anybody?).

Of all the minerals, zinc is the one most commonly used to bring about male sexual health. This is not to say that all a man needs to do is take zinc to have great sex—vites and mins are synergistic and you need them *all* working together in your body to bring about health, energy, and sexuality.

But zinc is concentrated in the prostate more than in any other part of the body. It's very important for males to take at least 50 mg a day for testosterone synthesis and the making of sperm, which obviously one needs to have a healthy and satisfying sex life. Some doctors recommend up to 50 mg of zinc three times a day after meals.

Vitamins A, C, and E, three strong antioxidants which strengthen the immune system, will work with the zinc to help eliminate prostate problems. I suggest 25,000 (minimum) units of beta carotene which is converted in the body into vitamin A, 3,000 mg (minimum) of vitamin C, and 400 units (minimum) of vitamin E. Chapter 7 has details of how much of all the vites and mins we all need plus how much I take every day.

Selenium is another antioxidant and a mineral that is extremely important to your prostate health, so be sure to look at the labels of any multi-vitamin you buy and see that all the above antioxidants are contained in it.

Men need sexual pleasure for other reasons besides pleasure; they need it for health reasons too. An orgasm is a release of tension and a flooding of the body with endorphins which flow through you and immediately make you feel good.

Now obviously a man needs not only his sexual apparatus to be healthy, he also needs the *rest* of his body to function at peak standards.

When your body is healthy, and you take good care of it, you will have a *natural* energy that never leaves you, and you'll go through life without anxiety or depression, but with a *natural* high!

7

You Can't Be Healthy and Be Impotent! You Can't Be Impotent and Be Healthy!

I learned something really interesting on my many TV and radio tours around the country. When I spoke about smoking being very bad for your health (I don't think there's anything worse!) and particularly bad for your heart and lungs, I'd never get any big call-in response from the radio listeners (and sometimes on particular TV shows, from viewers who could call in live).

But when I said (as I always did) that smoking was an almost certain end to sex-organ strength, the phone calls poured in. You see, almost everyone knows how bad smoke is for your lungs and how carcinogenic it is, and almost everyone knows how smoke causes free radicals to increase and do irreparable damage to your heart and lungs, *but* not everyone knows how smoke can seriously curtail your sexual activities and pleasure.

It literally can render you impotent!

Over thirty million American men have had some degree of impotence making them unable to achieve erection for intercourse. Most (but certainly not all) impotence happens to those over the age of fifty, and the cause for most of these men is cardiovascular disease. One of the culprits (besides animal fats and lack of exercise) is smoking.

Many people think cigs are relaxants, but they're not. They're stimulants, and when we smoke, the nicotine constricts our blood vessels and makes them so much smaller that the blood has a harder time getting through, *particularly* when there is plaque and/or other debris clinging to the sides of our blood vessels.

Now the swelling of the blood vessels in his penis is what gives a man an erection. The swelling also brings with it great sexual excitement. And the inhaled carbon monoxide reduces the blood oxygen and hormone production. The lung capacity is cut down and with it the ability for an erection to last during intercourse.

Every man is different and some male smokers don't start having problems till their forties and others can start in their early thirties. But eventually any and all smokers who have not succumbed to heart or lung problems will have sexual problems.

The AMA's Thomas Houston is quoted: "Tobacco is the only product in the U.S. that, when used as directed by the manufacturer, predictably kills the user."

I was on Morton Downey Jr.'s TV show several times and he's not only a wonderful TV host, he's a very loving and warm person. I remember discussing smoking with him in the makeup room before the show (I needed a gas mask), and he was far in denial about harming himself, and because I like him so much I was terribly sad knowing that he, being a heavy smoker, would soon either have a heart attack or get cancer.

When the inevitable happened recently and he was operated on successfully for cancer, he did a 180-degree turn and started warning everyone how dangerous cig smoke is.

What a shame we usually have to wait till the damage is done to see the harm, but better late than never. Once you stop smoking, the nicotine and tar is cleaned out of the body in a few months.

It's difficult, believe me I know. It's the toughest thing I've *ever* given up. Dieting and giving up foods is easy compared to stopping smoking. But the results are phenomenal. Your whole body starts to function better, from your eyesight to your breathing to your sex life.

And don't ever feel that because you've been smoking all your life that it won't make any difference if you stop, that all the damage has already been done.

That's not true. Your lungs will go back to their pre-smoking condition a few months after you stop.

And your sexuality will *also* go back to your pre-smoking condition. You'll get erections faster and easier, your PQ (pleasure quotient!) will go way up, and you'll make your mate a very happy woman.

Because this is a chapter all about and for men, I didn't mention that everything I said about smoking constricting the blood vessels in the penis also is true for the clitoris (the female penis). So women who smoke can be impotent too. If the woman's sex organs are not swelling and being engorged with blood, she's also not being aroused and her clitoris is not being sexually excited.

So if both of you are smokers, you're eventually going to have very little sex!

Liquor can also be deadening to the sex organs. Particularly if you overdo it and/or do it often. *All* drugs are bad for all your cells throughout your body. Cocaine, marijuana, speed, tranquilizers, antidepressants, and blood pressure medications are all drugs that alter your sexual appetite and sexual apparatus.

More than a million prescriptions are being given to patients each month for depression. The gigantic use of Prozac began in 1993 when Dr. Peter Kramer wrote *Listening to Prozac* which became a bestseller. Then in 1995 Dr. Peter Breggin wrote *Talking Back to Prozac,* in which he likens Prozac to amphetamines, and very much like speed, it boosts the level of serotonin (a neuro-transmitter) in the brain. Serotonin gives you a feeling of great energy and confidence. Most neurotransmitters act on only certain areas of the brain, whereas serotonin is found everywhere in the brain, including the places relating to sex. Prozac destroys the three phases of sex— desire, arousal, and orgasm. If anyone is taking Prozac or any other antidepressant (not including GH3), I sincerely urge you to read Dr. Breggin's great book. And if you'd like to know more about GH3 (the late Dr. Ana Aslan's great formulation for depression which has *no side effects),* read my last book, *GOOD IS ALIVE AND WELL AND LIVING IN EACH ONE OF US.* Also in this book I go into detail about many of the strongest antioxidants which I take every day.

St. John's Wort (hypericum perforatum) found in most health food stores, is widely prescribed in Europe, and has been proved in many clinical trials to have antidepressant activity equal to that of Prozac and other synthetic antidepressant drugs (which *all* have serious side effects ranging from anxiety attacks to impotence, and of course St. John's Wort has *no* side effects). Take it four times a day in the form of an extract which has 0.2 to 1.0 mg of hypericum, or a 500 mg capsule of the dried herb. The reason drug companies don't market GH3 or St. John's Wort is that they can't be patented, so there's no gigantic money to be made. Prozac made over one *billion* dollars ($1,200,000,000) for Eli Lilly in one year, and—hold everything!—now comes in peppermint flavor for the hundreds of thousands of kids now taking it. *Un*-believable!

So to have a robust sex life with your beloved, your body must be in good shape. Your sexual organs are a true barometer of your overall health, and if they're not functioning the way you'd like, look to what you're putting into your body.

In two of my previous books, *Everything You've Always Wanted to Know About ENERGY, but Were Too Weak to Ask,* and *Isle of View (Say it out loud),* I go into depth in layman's terms about all the vitamins and minerals, what they are and how they work, how much you should take and where you find them, so I decided not to go into detail again. I also tell about the John Ellsworth Hayden Foundation (named after my late father) giving away free *Dynamite energy shake®* to institutions (prisons, mental health institutes, old age homes, youth centers) where people obviously can't get out to buy the Dynamite at health stores. All this information is in either of those two books.

I have never made any money from the sale of the shake because taking it totally changed my life around from being a physical and mental wreck to being the healthiest, most energetic person I know. This is my way of showing my gratitude for having been led to invent the *Dynamite energy shake®*.

The only two vitamins you should not take too much of are vitamins A and D, and certainly the amounts I take are very safe and *far* under what could possibly be toxic, but more than the USRDA, which is ridiculously low. All the B vites and vitamin C are water-soluble, and if you ever did get a surplus, it would be flushed right out of your system. And your nervous system would sure be in good shape with all those Bs!

I formulated the *Dynamite vites*® for myself, and I take them every morning with my *Dynamite energy shake*®, but I couldn't make the tablets as potent in vitamins A and E as I wanted for myself because, for instance, if a person has a problem like high blood pressure (I don't), he or she should not take more than 400 units of vitamin E a day (which is the amount in the *Dynamite vites*®). I want 2,400 units a day, so I take 2,000 units *extra* of vitamin E and 12,000 mg *extra* vitamin C (everyone needs a different amount of vitamin C, and *my* requirements are very high).

It's up to each one of us to find the right amount of vitamin C that we need, and the barometer is stronger collagen and *no more colds*. I haven't had a bruise, or *even one cold* in over twenty-five years. I *start* to get 'em, then zap 'em with huge amounts of vitamin C and *lots* of liquid (and I've taken as much as 50,000 mg of vitamin C and sometimes more throughout one day, always followed by a *lot* of water).

Vites & Mins	I take 4 table-spoons *Dynamite energy shake*®	I take 12 tablets Dynamite vites®
Vitamin A (Beta-carotene)	——	30,000 I.U.
Thiamine (Vitamin B_1)	25 mg	150 mg
Riboflavin (Vitamin B_2)	25 mg	150 mg
Niacin (Vitamin B_3)	125 mg	250 mg
Niacinamide (Vitamin B_3)	125 mg	250 mg
Calcium	1,000 mg	2,000 mg
Iron	25 mg	36 mg
Vitamin B_6	25 mg	150 mg
Folic acid	400 mcg	800 mcg
Vitamin B_{12}	100 mcg	200 mcg
Iodine	210 mcg	300 mcg
Magnesium	560 mg	800 mg
Zinc	50 mg	30 mg
Copper	2 mg	4 mg
Biotin	300 mcg	600 mcg
Pantothenic acid	100 mg	300 mg
PABA	100 mg	300 mg
Choline	1,000 mg	1,000 mg

Inositol	1,000 mg	1,000 mg	
Potassium	1,000 mg	198 mg	
Papain	100 mg	200 mg	
Selenium	100 mcg	200 mcg	
Ribonucleic acid	100 mg	200 mg	
Betaine	100 mg	200 mg	
Molybdenum	100 mcg	——	
Chromium	100 mcg	200 mcg	
Vanadium	100 mcg	——	
Manganese	3 mg	10 mg	
Vitamin C	——	3,000 mg	(I take 12,000 mg extra)
Vitamin D	——	3,000 I.U.	
Vitamin E	——	400 I.U.	(I take 2,000 units extra)
Phosphorous	——	200 mg	
Citrus bioflavanoids	——	100 mg	
Glutamic acid	——	200 mg	

One of the reasons why the *Dynamite energy shake®* is so important for older people is the calcium. Younger people all need it too, but older people *urgently* need calcium so they won't have brittle and porous bones that break easily as they mature.

And actually the bones are the *last* parts of the body that lose calcium. When you're not getting enough calcium in your diet, which then leads to a calcium deficiency, the nervous system and the skin and other nonvital body parts are the *first* places that lose precious calcium.

So when your bones start to become brittle and porous, you must realize your body has already lost calcium and that's why you're tense, nervous, and not sleeping well. Four tablespoons of the *Dynamite energy shake*® in any liquid (juice or water) *gives the calcium equivalent of a quart of milk!* And it is so delicious in six different flavors that you'll find it hard to believe that anything that tastes that good can be that good for you!

The ginkgo tree is the longest-surviving living species of tree on earth, growing during the dinosaur era 250 million years ago, and it survived the Ice Age in Asia. As far back as 4800 years ago (2800 B.C.) the Chinese treated memory loss and poor circulation with this herbal mixture.

Ginkgo biloba is made up of flavanoid glycosides (a part of the bioflavanoid family), which benefit circulation, keep the capillaries from becoming brittle, aid the healing process, and have an anti-inflammatory action.

It's also made up of ginkgolides, which work synergistically with the flavanoids to reduce inflammation, and prevent the clumping of blood cells, which can lead to clots, which could cause a stroke or heart attack.

Then in 1985 a German study was done with sixty patients, fifty-seven to seventy-seven years old, and they all showed some mental deterioration. The researchers stated that the ginkgo biloba extract had a positive effect on the deterioration of mental performance and that this was reflected in the patients' behavior.

I've been taking it for over two years, and I can see a difference in my memory (which was awful when I was twenty and it's *still* awful, but getting better). It seems that because ginkgo helps the circulation it can be a brain stimulant, and being an antioxidant, it neutralizes free radicals before they can do their damage.

I take two dropperfuls of the almost tasteless liquid ginkgo biloba in a glass of water twice a day. It's recommended to take 30 mg of ginkgo from one to three times a day.

When I got back from my TV and radio tour of the South, there was a tiny package waiting for me in New York. It was an audiocassette sent to me by a listener of the Scoot Paisant show in New Orleans, and it told all about Pycnogenol, something about which I knew nothing. After listening to the tape, I ordered some and it's great. It's fifty times stronger than vitamin E and twenty times stronger than vitamin C in their antioxidant strength, but it works *with* them and magnifies their power.

CoQ10 is manufactured in the body and found in

some foods, particularly polyunsaturated oils. It's an essential substance in cell respiration, electron transfer, and the control of oxidation reaction. It works in the transport of electrons from the inside to the outside of cell membranes, is necessary for energy production, and is an antioxidant acting as a free-radical scavenger and protecting cell membranes from their damaging actions.

CoQ10 has helped heart ailments, increased muscle strength, improved gum tissue, helped with the synthesis and secretion of insulin, and in animals restored some of the age-induced decline of the immune system.

I heard about it through my late friend Herb Bailey, a medical researcher and writer of many health books, and started taking it about six years ago. I take three small capsules of 10 mg each after every meal, so I get 90 mg a day.

One of the most important things I learned from Herb was about SOD (superoxide dismutase), a protein—an enzyme found in all body cells—whose function is to fight the aging effects of superoxides (the medical term for free radicals) in the body—and the body is constantly creating these awful by-products.

These free radicals are oxygen molecules that lack one molecule, making them unstable, which starts their degenerative work.

Dismutation (deactivation) is what the SOD does

by transferring the free radical into stable oxygen and hydrogen peroxide. This prevents irreparable cell attack and damage, which causes rapid aging and deterioration.

I've been taking two SOD pills every morning with a glass of water an hour before my *Dynamite energy shake*®, and all my other vites and mins, to help keep me strong, energetic, and healthy.

I've always been a big fan and user of dolomite, a natural combination of calcium and magnesium in the best proportion of two to one. I'm repeating this because I feel it's *really* important for you to know about this healthy and natural relaxant. Whenever stress creeps up on me because of time (a deadline for something) or money (a late bill), I chew three or four dolomite pills, (after which I drink a glass of water), and if that's not enough, I take three or four more. In a matter of minutes I start to feel tension draining out and relaxation setting in.

I like 'em so much, in fact, that I've formulated something delicious called Dolomints®, which are minty and yummy. I am packaging them two ways: in large and small bottles, and like Lifesavers® so you can carry them in your purse or pocket and know that you're doing something good (and healthy) for yourself to relieve stress.

For SOD, call Gero Vita Int'l. at 1-800-406-1314.

Dynamite energy shake®,
Dynamite vites®, and Dolomints®
available in most health food stores or call
1-800-255-1660.

All other natural supplements in this book are
available at health food stores.

So drink eight to twelve glasses of water a day,
take lots of vites and mins, lots of antioxidants, some
exercise, little or no booze, *no* cigs or other addictive
drugs, and you'll be amazed at how speedy your sexual
recovery will be.

And how quickly your self-esteem will climb when
you're able to give the woman you love several orgasms
in intercourse (and you know she's not faking cause
you're *making* it happen for her)!

Sexual happiness is one of the greatest joys of love
and marriage ...

8
Why Marriage Is as Important to a Man as to a Woman

I learned a lot from my sex survey of married men. I'd always heard that statistically marriage is good physically, socially, and psychologically for men, but I'd never observed that firsthand.

When I got the results of the survey back I was surprised by some of the answers, but really surprised by the answers to "Why did you get married?"

Some men said "Because I fell in love," some said "Because it was time," but let me give you some other answers that I find enlightening.

- "Because I was very lonely living alone."
- "I never ate regular meals because I didn't care or take the time to cook for myself and I was sick a lot."

- "Because it was very stressful always having to come up with a date for the weekend."
- "I felt sad 'cause I didn't think anybody loved me and feeling loved is important to me. My wife loves me."
- "I lived with several girls over a period of four years and I still felt lonely with them (one for three months, one for two and a half years, and one for a little over a year). When I met my wife we had so much in common (which I didn't have with the other three, I just had sex on-call), I knew I wanted to spend my life with her."
- "I used to hang out with my buddies a lot and I wasn't as happy as I thought I should be. I was bored a lot and when I met my wife life became more exciting."
- "I went out with a different girl every nite (sic) and had sex with each one (this was before AIDS) and it was fun but something was missing and that was love. I found it with my wife."
- "I worked hard at my job and didn't have time to meet girls so I was lonely and didn't take very good care of my health which my wife does now."

An interesting statistic is that once men have been married, most divorced and widowed men remarry. The marriage rate for both is higher than the marriage rate for single men. Half of all divorced men remarry within three years.

So once a man experiences the feelings of intimacy, (even though it's not always a *deep* intimacy), and the knowledge that someone not only loves him but wants to take care of him physically, mentally, emotionally, and spiritually, those feelings of being loved are hard to resist and almost impossible to live without, the same as food and water.

Men (as do women) instinctively want to be stress-free and have fun as often as possible, and in a good relationship being loved brings hugs and kisses and sex and home-cooked food and fun.

Some men say they're afraid of marriage so they choose to live with different women, and it appears they're very happy with this noncommitted arrangement. I know a very important man in the music business, the CEO of a giant worldwide conglomerate, who lived with two different women over a period of eleven years (five and a half years each, just missing the common law statute which was probably deliberate). Then he lived with another woman for three years, and she was sure that she was the one to marry him. But alas, the moment he met a friend of mine, a darling PR woman, he fell madly in love, got the three-year relationship to move out, and he married his "true love."

Sometimes it does work out that people living

together finally tie the knot, but too many times it doesn't.

When love hits a man, I mean HITS a man, he wants *her* commitment, he wants to make sure that she is *his* woman, and that's what marriage does. It makes two commitments. And you let the whole world know "This is *my* man" and "This is *my* woman."

All insurance companies know that the health of a married man is much better than that of his single buddy. And it's the truth.

Marriage brings friendship, a relaxed atmosphere, steady sex, normal eating patterns and hours, and being needed by someone you love—the things that make a man healthier than life without them.

Milton Mayeroff in his book *On Caring* says,

The man who is not needed by someone . . . does not belong and lives like a leaf blown about in the wind.

As I mentioned earlier, all the years I was publicizing my little red marriage manual, *HOW TO SATISFY A WOMAN EVERY TIME* . . . *and have her beg for more!* everybody used to ask me when I was going to write *HOW TO SATISFY A MAN EVERY TIME* . . . *and have him beg for more!*

And every time someone did ask me, from three waiters and a captain who work at The Four Seasons restaurant in New York to Richard Bey on his fabulous syndicated TV show, I'd always give the same answer:

> Well, you don't know this, but I've already written it (at this I got a nice reaction). It's a very small book, actually it only has one page (at this everybody looked at me strangely) and at the top of the page are needed only two words to satisfy a man: Show up!

That always got a big laugh which was fun for me because I never made up a joke before and I loved making people laugh.

But then I started thinking about why so many men cheat, and it must be because sex at home isn't that exciting, and how important *exciting* sex is in life to men.

Then I started thinking about how many unhappy marriages there are and how many divorces, and if the men were really sexually happy in their marriages, they would do *anything* to keep those marriages going. Now true, many divorces are precipitated by the wives, but even if it's 50/50 wives and husbands, half the husbands are sexually dissatisfied enough to probably seek sex outside their marriages and eventually to divorce.

So even though most healthy men have only to *see* an attractive woman to become aroused, and they have an easy time reaching orgasm, there must be a reason why so many men who obviously were in love enough with their wives to have *married* them, are fooling around, having affairs, just all-around cheating, which almost always leads to the end of marriages. Cheating sexually is the real barometer that sex with spouse-o has gotten boring and won't last much longer.

One of my favorite examples is George and Nena O'Neill, who wrote *Open Marriage* a few years ago. I remember watching them on TV and hearing them on radio telling how they both had outside sexual partners and how it really worked to keep their marriage strong.

I never believed it and *knew* their marriage could never last. Then about three years ago I saw a story in the *New York Times* that George and Nena O'Neill had gotten a divorce.

Of *course* open marriage can't work. The most intimate part of marriage is being shared with outsiders, the pleasure bond of sexual excitement is being given to someone other than the spouse. How could any trust ever survive knowing that if she sees an attractive guy she'll probably seduce him and if he sees a hot-looking babe he'll bed her? Why be married? What's the point? Why not stay single and have each other as friends and keep sex out of it. Obviously the sex isn't exciting enough with each other to want to keep it just between them.

That *is* the point.

When sex is truly exciting, psychologically and physically (they *always* go together when sex is exciting, they *must* go together for sex to be exciting, and they are *always* together when two people first fall in love) then the point is to *keep* that excitement there throughout your marriage.

Now obviously everyone would *like* that to happen, but when it happens so incredibly seldom (like .0000000001 of 1 percent), we begin to doubt it's even possible to happen in a long-term relationship. Isn't that why people cheat, to have sex with someone new who promises to be exciting? Of course if you married her/him, it would probably get dull after a while too. And usually (but not always) does.

So it's the newness that seems to make it exciting. Well, if that were really true, the only answer to having exciting sex would be to constantly change partners.

Now there are some men who will possibly never cheat on their wives. Of course for the "in love" husbands, there's no desire or *reason* to cheat, but for all the others, it's not because they wouldn't like to, it's because the opportunity hasn't presented itself. Some men will never be the aggressor because they're so filled with fear or guilt, and this could be religious guilt and/or subconscious fears, which can and will paralyze a person through these negative emotions. And of course the fear that his wife will find out is always there.

But if another woman senses a man's need and desire (which would be emanating from him) she might make a move if she liked him. And if she did, he would respond if he believed that no one would ever find out. There's no man alive who, although he loves his wife, is not "in love" with her, won't have a secret affair if the circumstances are right.

So when I say there are some men who will maybe never cheat, it isn't that the thought hasn't crossed their minds, it's only that in each case no woman has let it be known to him that she is interested in having him as a lover.

Recently a friend of mine said to me that psychological problems, not lack of exciting sex, cause cheating and divorce. He said I was putting too much emphasis on the importance of sex in keeping a couple together. And I answered that psychological problems cause fear, lack of trust, anger at spouse, etc., and these negative emotions destroy sexual desire. Fear, lack of trust, and anger are not conducive to sexual intimacy and when sexual intimacy leaves a marriage, the "marriage" is over. The relationship might continue because she's afraid of being alone and he needs the security of having someone take care of him, etc., but the union of two-people-as-one is over. They are now two separate people living under the same roof, and they may love each other as friends, but the deep intimacy is over.

I also believe that the dynamics of sexual pleasure are so powerful that no matter what psychological problems a married couple may have (he's a compulsive gambler, a liar, a thief, etc.), if they love and respect each other enough to focus on and keep the sex exciting between them, the marriage will endure.

Now comes the complex part. Can a man who is a compulsive gambler (drinker, etc.) respect *himself* enough to love and respect his wife? If he's "out of control" (as a gambler or alcoholic obviously is), *could* he respect himself? Self-respect comes from inner strength and a compulsive gambler (drinker, etc.) is not as strong as his compulsion. If he were, he'd be able to control it, and he cannot. So without self-respect there can't be other-respect, and without respect for the other, real love cannot exist and grow. *Need* can exist, but not love.

But he *could* love her enough to be afraid of losing her, and he *could* make a decision to change himself so that his self-respect would strengthen because he overcame a compulsion, and his respect and love for his wife would grow in the same ratio as his own self-respect.

I know a woman who fell in love with an alcoholic and he with her. After about three months she gave him an ultimatum: stop drinking or I'm leaving you. She kept her word and left, and four days later he called her and said he couldn't live without her, and vowed never to drink again, and he never did. They've been happily married for over thirty years.

So when it comes to psychological problems, which

many of us have, it really depends on how strong our love of spouse is, how strong our negative compulsion or neurosis is, and if our inner strength is enough to overcome the negative so that our self-love and spouse-love will thrive.

But although most of us don't have *major* compulsions and neuroses, we do have minor ones. And the physical pleasure of sex is so strong that it will overcome just about anything and everything, and bring a couple closer together every time they share the intimacy of each giving the other the gift of an orgasm.

And what about physical problems where the husband's libido is dulled by medication or drugs? Even these problems don't totally stop a man from some form of sexual pleasure, usually masturbation.

Most husbands masturbate. The only ones who don't are those whose wives take care of them sexually every day. Even those who drink too much or who are on other drugs, masturbate. With those not in great health it doesn't happen every day or every few days like those who don't take any stimulants, tranquilizers, high blood pressure medication, sleeping pills, or other toxic substances. But unless he is almost comatose, it does happen, if only once a week or once a month.

The bottom line is that every man who is not "in love" with his wife (although he may still love her) will have an affair if he's healthy enough and the opportunity presents itself.

But the real thrill and happiness of life is when a man and a woman fall in love, marry, and stay ''in love'' as long as they live.

In Mia Farrow's great book, *What Falls Away,* she writes about working with Roman Polanski while he directed her in *Rosemary's Baby.* She recounts how one day while waiting to shoot, Roman was saying that long-term monogamy was impossible because a man's sexual attraction for one woman only lasts a short time. John Cassavetes, the late actor-writer-director, was also in the film working as an actor, and he very excitedly told Roman that Roman knew little or nothing about women or relationships, and that he, John, was more attracted now to his wife Gena Rowlands then he ever was since they got married years before. Mia writes that Roman was so taken aback by John's outburst that he could only stare at him, then he blinked at him a few times, and had no reply.

Arnold Schwarzenegger was interviewed in *Cosmo* about his marriage, as were several other actors, and they all stated how important their wives were to them and how much better their lives are since they've been married.

Arnold said that when he grew up in Austria his mother took care of his father and cooked and looked after their house, and that's the kind of woman Arnold thought he'd marry. But when he finally did fall in love and married Maria Shriver he got much more than just a wonderful care-giver as his mother was, he also got an exciting career woman.

Denzel Washington is so thrilled with marriage and his wife Pauletta, that he married her twice so that she and the world would know how happy he is and how much he loves her after a decade and a half of being together.

Suzanne Fields, a syndicated columnist in the *New York Post,* had an article titled ''When Marriage Is the Food of Love,'' and in it she quotes Leon Kass, a professor of social thought at the University of Chicago, ''Marriage is not something one tries on for size and then decides to keep,'' writes Kass in a provocative essay in *The Public Interest.* ''It is rather something one decides with a promise and then bends every effort to keep.''

Ms. Fields goes on to tells us that living together doesn't do what it proposes to do. She says it's a fact that couples who live together and then marry have a higher percentage of divorce than those who don't live together before they get married.

''Sex cuts into the friendship stage, which can provide the basis for a long-lasting marriage. Passion quickly fulfilled reduces the need for commitment, the need to sacrifice something of oneself in the tender trap of marriage.

She continues that men, anxious to try any woman's sexual favors, hardly ever pursue depth in friendship with them. She quotes Rousseau: "Men will forever strive to please women, but only if someone exerts control over their sexual power and sets the standards for that pleasing."

Then she says that with encouragement, young people can channel their desires into the "slower rituals of self-restraint in courtship."

In a wonderful article in *Cosmo,* Keith Blanchard explains "Why Men Secretly Want to be Given the Big Ultimatum." He states that "Marriage isn't just a rubber-stamped version of living together—it's a quantum leap into a new existence." He says that in his case, after getting married: "Beyond all expectation, my life is immeasurably richer, with a fulfilling complexity I was unable to imagine."

My late aunt, Phyllis McGinley, who won not only the Pulitzer Prize for her wonderful book *Times Three,* she also won the very prestigious Laetare Medal of the Catholic church. *Times Three* is a compilation of three decades of her brilliant, clever, warm, and always witty poetry about marriage. Aunt Phyllis and Uncle Bill were happily married for many years, and I think she summed up connubial bliss very well when she wrote:

In a successful marriage, there is no such thing as one's way. There is only the way of both, only the bumpy, dusty, difficult, but always mutual path!

I agree with Aunt Phyllis, and the reason why marriage is as important to men as it is to women is because men have the same emotional need to be loved as women do, and both are overtly seeking and searching for the same togetherness and the same soul mates to walk with down that mutual path.

So even though some men yell and scream that marriage is only for women, and make with the jokes that "My wife is married, I'm not!" and call the "little woman" a "ball and chain," the statistics prove that marriage *is* as important to men as it is to women, possibly more so.

9

The Master Plan: How to Keep Your Husband Happy and Faithful Forever . . .

The most important part of marriage is love. But again, the deepest *expression* of that love is sex. Certainly you can hold hands and hug and kiss, but sex is the closest two people can ever get emotionally, mentally, spiritually, and obviously physically. Two people can't *get* any closer physically than intercourse.

So to have a happy marriage the first ingredient is love. And part of that love is like. It is *not* a cliché to say your spouse should be your best friend.

To have a lasting relationship you must have interests in common and you must like the person you're sexually attracted to. If you love movies and don't particularly like theater and your spouse hates flicks and adores stage plays, you're going to have to compromise a lot. If you love the shore and your beloved likes the desert, you love rock and spouse-o loves classical, there's gonna be a *life* of compromise.

Again, let me bring up Donald Trump, who was quoted on the TV show *E.T.* about his separation from Marla:

> Marla is not a person that's into the world of the materialistic, as perhaps I am. She would rather walk down the beach for three hours than make 400 calls to bankers and associates and people like I have to, and I would rather make the phone calls.

I believe that the reason they didn't see (or didn't care to see) that they had little in common was because Donald, like most husbands in long-term marriages, was probably so bored sexually and was so turned-on by the exciting sex with his new amour, that nothing else mattered but to continue with the exciting sex. And the exciting sex led to their getting married. As I see it, once the sexual *excitement* died down, the important differences in their personalities—he craving action and she craving peacefulness—became more obvious and less acceptable to him.

So don't go to bed with every person of the opposite sex you meet 'cause sex is very persuasive when it comes to making a commitment, and you can believe you're "in love" when what it *really* is is "in lust," and after a while you may find out you actually had *nothing* in common.

When reality sets in you may find you are almost total opposites, and even though opposites may attract, they sure don't stay together.

We want to be with someone who has our same sense of humor (boy, is *that* important!), our same values, our same sensitivities, plus all the other sames.

Peter Falk fell in love with and married Shera Danese because he says she makes him laugh, and Johnny Depp says of his sweetie, Ms. Moss, "Kate makes me laugh!"

But once you've met someone special whom you truly like, and you have lots of sames, and you go to bed and sex is divine, *that's* the person to spend your lifetime with.

There's a well-known quote that I *don't* agree with:

> When sex is great, it's ten percent of
> a marriage.
> When sex is bad, it's ninety percent
> of a marriage.

The bad sex being ninety percent, I agree with, but when sex is great, it's *also* ninety percent of a marriage to a man. It may be less important to a wife, but it's ninety percent important to a husband. The reason sex is ever "bad" is because when your spouse starts taking you for granted and doesn't really pay attention to you, sex gets boring. A man will not marry a woman if he's not sexually attracted to her (unless of course he's marrying her for her money or if it's an arranged marriage).

So the love is there (or you wouldn't have gotten married), and hopefully the like is also there and you're really compatible, and when you have all the rest, great sex can make you put up with a lot of sass and problems that two people living together *always* encounter that might otherwise overwhelm your relationship.

Now remember, sex is the closest two people can ever get, so great sex is the deepest expression of your love for each other. One of the main reasons why sex gets boring later on in a marriage is because one or both of the partners are bored sexually. The excitement has died because you've allowed yourselves to forget the "sexual master" part of sex. Once a husband learns how to give her an orgasm through intercourse alone (he takes charge of her body), she'll want sex as much and as often as he does! And she'll do *anything* for him sexually to make it exciting to assure he'll continue giving her the greatest orgasms she's ever had. And once a wife takes charge of his body, he'll do anything for her.

Because this book is a marriage manual, I have to assume you love your spouse. Maybe sex has gotten boring, but you still love each other. When you first dated, you were very sexually attracted to each other and when you made love (assuming you did before you got hitched), the sex was phenomenal. Just being near each other got you excited and you both started really feeling like you were ''in love.''

That's why you wanted to get married. You, the husband, liked her of course, but the sexual excitement was overpowering and you wanted to make love to her *forever!*

Did you ever wonder *why* you were was so much in love? Didn't you feel that she was in charge of you sexually? She was the one who really turned you on, you were charged up every time you were near her and you got incredibly excited thinking about going to bed with her, but she was the one who had to say OK. She was in control of the sex, and you were dependent on her and her body to make you surrender in an orgasm.

She was like your sexual master inasmuch as she had the power within her body and her mind to get you and keep you excited, and then she had to *respond* to you and your desires before you could have an orgasm. Well, you could have masturbated and *thought* about her, but that's not real surrender even though your fantasies of her may have played a big part.

There's no mystery with masturbation, no surprises. How *could* there be? *You're* the one in charge! How could you *not* know what you're going to do?

So for masturbation (vs. intercourse), there is no surrender, no master, only fantasy.

To have real sexual surrender (again, that's what a perfect total orgasm is!) takes a person you really love and trust and are turned on by. And you're *never* turned on by someone you feel is beneath you or weaker than you, or dumber than you. A man wants a woman who's strong and who *knows* she's in charge of him, and who's really focused on him, really paying attention to him, really crazy about him, and that's what you had when you were dating.

During the dating phase, even if a woman doesn't have an orgasm, she'll fake it (as I did too many times) because she loves him and wants to have a permanent relationship with him and she instinctively knows how important sex is to a man. So the sex wasn't that great for her (I'm talking intercourse), and after you got married she stopped being your ''sexual master,'' she stopped consciously using her power over you, and sex started slowly getting less exciting for you till it started getting actually boring.

That's the point at which most men start looking around and fooling around. It could be after twenty years, or eight years, or two years—it all depends on the man and his boredom/excitement threshold to how quickly he will cheat. There's *nothing* deadlier to a marriage than boring sex.

Now we all know sex is never boring but the person sexing you is boring, so he's gonna find *another* exciting woman who *will* turn him on.

But he doesn't have to!

The woman he's married to can once again assume her power and become his sexual master and take charge of his body.

It can't be just *one* of the partners who is in charge all the time. That would be constantly exciting for the recipient of the sexual master making him or her have an orgasm every time, but it would soon become *very* boring for the one in charge *always* to be in charge.

So what you have to do is take turns. One time one of you is in charge, is the sexual master and drives the other crazy with not knowing when (or if!) you'll make him or her have an orgasm, and the next time the other spouse does the same.

What you're going to learn in this book, the very most important thing, is that the psychological and the technical/physical part of lovemaking are equally important. How you physically make love to him must show him that you have taken charge of his body. A woman who grabs his penis and squeezes it hard and bites it, then grabs his balls till they hurt, is not in charge, she's a roughneck. The woman who first looks at his penis, then gently takes it, tenderly licks it and brings hcr tongue down to his balls and gently runs her tongue over them and goes back to his penis and runs her tongue over the top, gently sucking the tip, that woman is in charge of his body and really *loves* his body, and he knows it!

She has taken over his psyche!

You, the wife, when you take charge of his body, are going to *make* him have an orgasm after sweetly teasing him and driving him crazy with his not knowing *when* you're going to make him come or even *if* you're going to make him come.

You're going to have fun with him and play the game of sex. And it is fun to be in charge of somebody's body and have the power to give him an orgasm when and if you decide the time is right.

A little sweet, loving torture is a *big* turn on!

Remember:

> Sex is *always* a game!
> Love is *never* a game!

You never tease with love. You always tease with sex.

Teasing really turns a woman on when her husband drives her wild with physical promises of orgasm that he deliberately keeps lovingly withholding till she's absolutely crazy with desire.

And as exciting as that is for a female, it's just as exciting to a man to have his woman take charge of *his* body and drive him wild by sexually teasing him and then giving him the greatest orgasm he's ever had in his life.

When you do decide you're going to take charge of your husband's body, you should tell him just before he leaves for work, or call him at work, that *tonight* is the night you're going to take complete control of his body and tease him till he goes out of his mind. Let him think about it all day.

And when he comes home, lead him to the bedroom and slowly take off his shirt, belt, slacks, undershirt, and underwear, and tell him to lie on the bed.

Slowly start to take *your* clothes off, first your dress or blouse and skirt/pants, then your bra, and then your panties. Go over to him, and take both of your hands with your fingers extended and lightly run them over his chest and arms.

Tell him he's not allowed to move or to touch you, that's part of the deal of *you* taking charge. So tease his chest and arms and softly tease the inside of his thighs with the pads of your fingertips. Then tell him to bend his legs, and gently go with your fingertips behind his knees and tease him there.

At a certain point (and *you* are in control of whenever you want), gently touch his balls and tease them all over. Then go to his penis and gently run your fingers up and down it. Wet your fingertips and run them across the tip, and as he gets more aroused, go back down the shaft, then do the same thing with your tongue.

When he *really* gets hot, stop what you're doing with his penis and go back to teasing his chest and arms.

Do not let him touch you.

He must be passive because you are actively in control. You can continue going from teasing his arms and legs and nipples back to his penis. Start over again as many times and as long as you want. It's *your* game and *you* are the coach calling every play.

Something that is very sexy to your husband is for you to masturbate him with your hand.

Put either hand around his penis and begin to move it up and down as you play with it. If it's not already wet because you've been sucking it, put some saliva into your hand, or better yet give it a nice loving and very wet suck so it is slippery as your hand goes up and down.

Gently keep moving your hand up and down, and you can every once in a while put your mouth over the head of it, roll your tongue around it and gently suck it and lick it. Then go back to playing with it, keeping it wet and moving your hand up and down until he comes. I promise you he will love it.

Or, if you feel that after you have teased him with your mouth and hands, the time has come for you to give him an intercourse orgasm, you very gently climb onto his body, straddling him, and *slowly* lower yourself onto his penis, *very* slowly. When it's about half-way in, raise up a little, very slowly go in and out halfway down a few times, then slowly go all the way down.

You are still in charge, still on top, and he will erupt very soon. Just keep slowly going up and down on his penis till he explodes into your body with the most intense orgasm he's ever had.

Or, if you'd rather give him an oral orgasm, once you've got him really aroused, go back to his penis and start softly tongue-teasing it again, and then put your hand around it and start moving it up and down the slippery wet shaft. He will love it when you take control of his penis and make it harder and bigger by playing with it with your hand and at the same time sucking and licking the head of it, except this time you're going all the way to make him erupt into the greatest prolonged pleasure he's ever had. You move your hand to the base of his penis and begin to slowly and gently move your mouth up and down, your tongue gently going all over it. The sensation to your husband is that he's "fucking your mouth," and that is very exciting to him.

As you continue, very gently teasing his throbbing penis with your tongue, and gently sucking it, let it go tenderly in and out of your mouth, and as you feel him getting more and more excited, you can make your mouth tighter around it as you move your mouth up and down until he has an orgasm. And what an orgasm it will be. And what a sense of power and love you'll feel for the man you love.

Or, let's say you both have to get to work and you don't have much time, but you decide to give him a "quickie" and take charge of his body on the spur of the moment. Your husband is already in bed and you reach under the covers and gently take his penis in your hand and softly caress it. It starts to get hard, and you continue fondling as it grows bigger and harder.

Now you pull the covers back and softly put your mouth over the tip and very gently suck it. Then you run your tongue gently up and down the shaft, put it *all* in your mouth and suck it till he comes. That's a *real* quickie (about five minutes) and he'll love it.

But let's say you're not in a tremendous hurry, so you've got him where he's out of his mind with pleasure and probably seconds away from orgasm when you take your mouth away and begin to softly kiss the inside of his thighs.

You can gently whisper, "I'm not ready yet, sweetheart, to give you an orgasm." This will really stun him, because you have totally taken over his body. You are in charge and he knows it. "I'll let you know when I'm ready," you whisper.

After gently kissing the inside of his thighs, you might want to go back to his penis and tease a little more. The more you tease, the stronger the orgasm when he finally has it.

If you want to continue teasing, you might go to his nipples and very gently rub your tongue around the sides and very softly kiss them. And you might want to continue fondling him while you kiss his nipples.

By now he's fully crazed with desire, and you might feel you're ready to give him an orgasm. It's *your* call, so do whatever *you* feel you want to do, and he'll be so attuned to the fact that *you* took control, that *you* made him wait till *you* wanted him to have an orgasm.

What a turn-on to a guy to be *sometimes* passive.

The more fun you have with sex the better it always is. Maybe you'll get on top of him and use his penis to play with your own clit till *you're* crazy with desire. That is a *huge* turn-on to a man to know you're using his penis to masturbate and drive yourself crazy.

And maybe you'll actually give yourself an orgasm, rubbing your clit with his penis till you come, and then put it inside yourself and move up and down on it. Believe me, he won't be able to control himself and he will also orgasm as you move up and down.

Oral sex and woman-on-top are the two best ways for a woman to take charge of her husband's body. Man-on-top, aka intercourse missionary position, is the most exciting and satisfying sex to both a husband *and* a wife *only* if done with my new technique in *HOW TO SATISFY A WOMAN EVERY TIME* ... *and have her beg for more!*

One very exciting game (and lots of fun) is to *role-play*. In my 1981 sex survey of married women from which I based *HOW TO SATISFY A WOMAN EVERY*

<u>*TIME*</u> . . . *and have her beg for more!,* one of the women wrote an addendum on the back of one of the pages telling how she drove her husband wild by telling him that he was a "bad little boy" and wasn't allowed to touch any part of her body until he apologized, and even then she wouldn't let him go all the way until *she* felt appeased that he was really sorry for being so "bad."

I have taken her idea and dramatized it in a very sexy way:

After you have slowly taken all your clothes off in front of him and then slowly taken all his clothes off (when you're in charge, *you* do the undressing—when he's in charge, *he* will), you will begin the *real* fun. At first you play with his penis and get it big and hard and then say:

> You know, you've been a *naughty* boy and I don't know if I should let you touch me or not. I don't think we should make love," you tell him as you lie next to him on the bed. "I don't want to allow anyone as naughty as you to ever touch my body."
>
> As he stares at you in wonderment, you say, "Are you sorry you've been such a bad little boy?" and when he says "Yes" (which he *has* to say to continue), you ask him "Are you going to apologize for being so naughty? 'Cause if you don't, we're not going to make love."

And then you make sure he says "I'm sorry" and then make him say "I apologize."

"Okay, you apologized, would you like to touch my nipple just for a second?"

"Yes," and he touches it.

"Would you like to suck my nipples just for a minute?"

"Yes," and he puts his lips on one and sucks it for a few moments, then on the other one.

"Would you like to touch me where I'm all hot between my legs? But that's all a bad little boy can do, just touch it for a second," and he touches it with his hand.

Then you say, "I think I'm going to let you play with my pussy for a minute and get me hotter, but just for a minute."

He starts to softly (make sure to let him know you want it *gently)* play with your clit.

As you get more aroused (and he is already aroused), you say to him, "Because you've apologized, I'm going to let you put it in, but only a tiny bit—you can only put the head in and no more."

He gets on top and puts the head into you. And you say, "You did say you were sorry for being so naughty, so I'm going to let you go in another inch, but *no more* than that . . ."

"Okay, you can put it in a little bit more, but only go in halfway—that's all, just halfway."

"You know, I'm going to forgive you for being such a bad, naughty little boy and let you go in all the way, but very, *very* slowly."

And you keep it up till orgasms happen.

Now you can write any scenario you want. Remember, it's a game and you've gotta have fun. Maybe he'll play the young, shy delivery boy and you are the older, married woman hot for his young, hard body, and you have to seduce him. By asking him if he ever saw a woman's tits before, and you open your blouse and let him look at your bra, and ask him if he'd like to unhook your bra and touch your nipples, you can really get this "little kid" horny for you.

Maybe you'll be a young schoolgirl that he'll try to seduce, and he'll ask you to sit on his lap, and then he'll ask if you'll let him take your panties off, then he'll ask if he can touch your little pussy. By this time both of you (if you're really focusing on each other) will be hot.

Or maybe you're his teacher at school, he's a kid, and he tries to seduce you by asking if he can stay after school and talk to you. Then he tells you you're the prettiest teacher in the school and he dreams about you a lot. He tells you he's never thought about a woman's body until you, but now all he can think about is your body.

You could tell him he's naughty and you're going to have to spank him for talking like that (and that's what you do after you take his pants off), and then after he's spanked maybe you'll suck his penis till he goes crazy; or you could slowly take your blouse or sweater off, your skirt, and get down to your bra and panties, and tell him you're going to show him what you want him to do as his first lovemaking lesson. Anything you can imagine, you can play.

How could he *ever* get bored with all the girls and women you are inside yourself and will be teasing him with? Of course you can use wigs to *really* look like different women if you want, but they're not really needed because it's your *attitude* that's important. You can wear a schoolgirl dress or a hooker's G-string and panties, or a pseudo-leather outfit with a whip, or a riding habit with a riding crop.

The women you can become are *unlimited* (but you don't have to have any costumes if you have the right attitude!).

Or you can just use your imagination and your partner will never know how you're imagining hc's spanking you or that she's got you tied to the bed as she's licking all over your body, slowly getting closer to your penis.

To me, costumes are fun, but superfluous, because

if you use your imagination and really pretend you're someone else, it frees you. How can you be uptight if you go back in your memory and remember when you were seven years old, or eleven or fifteen? And each one of us has within us lots of different personalities that we have stifled because we were taught that it was inappropriate to act in many different ways.

But that's the secret to play-acting. An actor unlocks a different character and personality with each role he plays. Now you're not out to win an Academy Award, you're out to turn your spouse on. And as long as you believe you *could* be a schoolteacher seducing a young boy, that's all that's needed.

You can be shy, tough, innocent, sadistic (with your riding crop which you flick onto his behind). Once you both get into it, it's not only fun (because you're really not yourself anymore) but it's also sexy. You'll either be his sexual master or he'll be yours. And tomorrow or next week or later today, you'll reverse your roles.

Most of the time you may just want to have beautiful sex with your spouse without any games, and an amazing thing happens. You will remember whatever favorite role really turned you on, and you'll be making love to the *master* in that role, which is the same one that you were in love with when you first fell in love.

Whether you recognize it or not, each one of us is and always has been searching for someone we look up to, that person who has the power to control us. You can deny it, but in reality that's what you were to each other when you fell in love. And when you become each other's "sexual master" again, the tremendous excitement will start all over again.

It's all a game and *anything* goes!

Falling in love, being in love, and expressing that love in orgasms of mutual pleasure and profound love is the closest we will ever be to heaven on this plane. What a pity churches don't comprehend this and teach it, because if they did, married couples would be infinitely happier and much more likely to stay together. With that "pleasure bond" cementing them together and with a sense of fun, the sexual excitement, the love and the marriage will *all* last *"as long as you both shall live . . ."*

Afterword

To all you women out there who are putting into action what you have just read, and are with open hearts and much love and passion pleasuring your men . . .

thank you . . .

And to all you men out there who are no longer practicing THE BIG BANG THEORY, but are, with much love, gently and tenderly pleasuring your women . . .

thank you . . .

because from all of you who are giving and receiving and making love, lots of that love is spilling over and touching all the rest of us, and because we're all connected, when you're more loving it touches me, and when I'm more loving it touches you.

We're all in this together, and love makes us know we're all one.

NAURA'S OTHER BOOKS:**

HOW TO SATISFY A WOMAN EVERY TIME
. . . And Have Her Beg For More!
• A marriage manual and a marriage saver!
• This is the first and *only* book that shows a man *exactly* how
• *#1 Bestseller* 1992 Hardcover Nonfiction—*Publishers Weekly*
• 62 weeks *The New York Times* #1 bestseller 1992–1993
• ''It really works!''—*The Los Angeles Times*

Everything You've Always Wanted to Know About ENERGY . . . But Were Too Weak To Ask
• All about physical, mental, and emotional energy
• Over 2-million-copy bestseller
• On every bestseller list in the country

ISLE OF VIEW (Say It Out Loud)
• All about loving yourself and loving others
• "This upbeat book follows its predecessor onto the best-seller lists." —*Publishers Weekly*

GOOD IS ALIVE AND WELL AND LIVING IN EACH ONE OF US
• A revolutionary self-change* book
  *physically, mentally, emotionally and spiritually

ASTRO-LOGICAL LOVE
• A *logical* look at astrology!
• Do the simple charts in just minutes and find out all about personality and character traits of yourself and everyone else in your life.
• "Do a chart and find out about everyone you know." —*People*

THE HIP, HIGH-PROTE, LOW-CAL, EASY-DOES-IT COOKBOOK
• A vegetarian cookbook with over 200 delicious meatless recipes
• "Heartily recommended . . ." —King Features